HIGH
CRYSTAL

HIGH CRYSTAL

BY

Martin Caidin

ARBOR HOUSE
New York

F
Cai

for my redneck brother,
Jay Barbree

CHAPTER I

THE LIGHTNING exploded from Stygian blackness. Until this moment there had been only distant flashes, glowing the skies in great flickerings, painting ghostly veils of falling rain. The flashes gleamed and as quickly vanished, and where the six men in the high-winged transport had seen a touch of the storm, the visible world again became the deep-red glow and blue-white tiny pools of the instrument panel and the flight deck. But there was no question of the violence through which they tossed and stumbled, the long thin wings flexing wildly in turbulence, the mixed updrafts and sudden down-smashing blows of air making a mockery of control.

Six men knowing this could be their last flight. No question of their confidence in the big four-engined machine, the powerful turboprops, the sturdy structure. Tried, proven, the deep-bellied Hercules that had worn its name so well for so many years. This crew had flown this same iron bird through squall lines that shattered equipment, gales, thunderstorms, massive fronts, ice and snow and typhoon.

This storm was different. The airspeed needle swinging crazily from left to right, at one moment showing them in almost a full stall, the next instant a velocity great enough to bend metal. The climb rate swung from one stop to the other—a good thing it was indicating rate instead of actual climb or long before now the wings would have separated, the tail would have twisted, ripped away. Even the altimeter needle slipped across the edge of the normal world. Its indication most reflected the actual events. Flung aloft on a howling stream of air, they shot from 17,000 to some 25,000 feet, everyone clammed into his seat. Of a sudden they hurtled in the other direction, plunging toward the massive crags they knew were below. Up was more acceptable. The storm could throw you just so high and no more. It might spit the entire machine from one of its flanks, but beyond that was safety and smooth flight. Down was another matter. It could be lethal. They shot skyward then, a long moment of false calm, suspended, wings stripped naked of their lift. Just suspended between the forces of the storm; far below, to the sides and above, the ghostly orange-yellow lightning. They knew. Despite whirling propellers, powerful engines, their skill with the controls and their prayers and curses, they had to go down.

Their heads went tight with the sudden negative pressure. Lap belts and shoulder harnesses dug into flesh as they heaved upward from their seats. Oil and hydraulic pressure readings sagged or went to zero in the sudden negative gravity. Nose down, wings heeled over, the sickening plunge began as they rode an invisible monstrous falling river of air. All about them, ghostly radiance. Slight fingers of blue-white spitting from propellers, from the nose radome, the wingtips, glowing

10

about the big external tanks slung beneath the wings. Static electricity. St. Elmo's Fire. They were supercharged with electrical forces unable to discharge. They fell, helpless, and they were damn frightened. They watched the altimeter unwind, the rate of descent a warning they could not respond to. A long moment to stare at the yellowish glow of the radar scope, showing a world filled with splotches and crazy lines, telling them of the rivers of rain in front of them. But they already knew that. They ignored the water-filled sky and thought of their drop toward the mountains, bracing themselves for the shock when they broke free of the enormous downdraft and—

The lightning exploded at them from an unseen place within the greater storm. No time to see the huge bolt coming at them. Too fast. One instant it was not there, in the next blink it seemed all that existed. If they had had the vision to see what had come from powerful but invisible forces, they would have seen a rope of naked, raw energy—a rope of electrons, snapping from its point of generation to their metal craft; energy moving invisibly through air at some twenty-six thousand miles a second. And so it seemed to the relatively slow reflexes of the six men inside the laboring Hercules that one instant there was no lightning and in the next minuscule fraction of a heartbeat it was *there.*

No sound; not yet. Radiance beyond human measure bathed metal and cloth and flesh. Then the heat. Forty-five thousand degrees of it. Hotter than the surface of the sun. The reflex of pain mercifully lagged behind the impact of the energy bolt as it assaulted the metal intruder in this savaged space of air. One instant there was an airplane, in the next an explosion and a ball of flaming wreckage quickly shredded and flung away.

Storms are sometimes capricious. Five men died instantly. Not the sixth. Electrical energy flashed to his side, crashed between his legs, tore the flight jacket from his back, burned away his shoes and, in the space created when the airplane was sundered, exploded his body into the maw of the storm. He was falling, ejected from the airplane. No strong pain. Shock had nearly overwhelmed it. Also fear. The conditioning of training and experience came to the forefront of dim awareness.

What had happened to the big C-130E ... had to be lightning ... there was the blinding flash and—his mind went to the immediate: He was in the air. He was falling. He must react. They hadn't been that high above the ground. The infrared mapping pass was being flown at 22,000 feet. The peaks below could be anywhere from 7,000 to 19,000 feet. *Pull the D-ring. Don't waste time.* His right hand crossed his chest, grasped the metal handle, jerked. Above wind and storm he heard—imagined he heard?—and surely felt springs snap open, as the pilot chute leaped into the wind and dragged the chute behind. Then a sudden booming *crack* and a wild swing as the canopy blossomed and he was floating down through a maelstrom of wind and lightning and thunder.

Jagged lightning strikes through the air, exploding like huge flashbulbs to provide momentary vision, revealed the peaks of the Cordillera Vilcabamba as well as others no one had ever seen to the northeast of that range. He knew that swinging into those peaks in the high winds—and he could only estimate his speed across the ground at between twenty and thirty miles an hour—could mangle or kill him. He hoped he would descend to a lesser altitude. His only real chance was to reach the thick jungle—inhospitable as it might be, it was preferable to jagged rock. Another flicker of lightning. A thick carpet of trees loomed before him. But . . . he was puzzled for a moment, and then just before he hit he understood the tremendous speed of his descent. He still must be more than two miles above sea level and the air here was still thin and he was coming down too damned fast and—

He struck the upper branches of a tree with a ground speed of more than forty miles an hour. A sharp gnarled branch cracked the upper bone of his left arm as if it were a twig. He gasped with the pain that became worse as the parachute canopy snagged in the branches and jerked him almost to a stop before his legs struck the ground. Still, if the canopy had not caught he would have smashed into the ground with impact to break his back or fracture his skull, and the tree held the chute so that it did not billow before the powerful winds and drag him across the ground.

Pain dizzied him but experience and training stayed. With his right hand he released the clasp to separate the chute harness by his left shoulder, giving him some freedom of movement. Despite his helpless arm he managed to extricate himself from the rest of the harness. It was still a drenching rain and the wind at this altitude could freeze him to death within a few hours. He had no sure idea about where he was. Experience and training: *use them.*

He removed the survival kit from the bottom of the chute harness. A mercury-cell flasher showed the way to the base of a huge tree where he could sit. The medical kit. Morphine to cut the pain he knew would soon come from the arm. Before the drug hit there should be time to do the rest. Setting the two aluminum sheets from the kit for a splint was clumsy, an agony. He fashioned a sling from shroud lines cut away from the chute. He managed to force down an emergency ration bar for energy. His head reeled from mild shock, pain and the thin air at this altitude. He must be ten thousand feet or higher. He would need rest, sleep. The kit again. A mylar-insulated blanket. Weighed two ounces. He wrapped it about himself, tucked it in. Within minutes he was feeling warmer; the blanket retained 90 percent of his body heat. He formed a poncho over his head with the mylar, made a flap to protect his face from the rain.

He sat. Unable, despite the morphine, to sleep. It would

13

come slowly but it would come. Sitting with the rain hissing about him, the thunder, he remembered. . . . He had landed on a hard surface. Flat. He flicked on the flashlight, moved the beam slowly. He didn't believe it.

A road. *A highway.* In the midst of towering raw peaks and crags in a totally uninhabited high reach of the Peruvian Andes. Impossible. He studied the hard, solid surface. As far as the flashlight would throw its beam, before it was lost in the heavy rains, this impossible highway continued. Wonder faded before the onset of morphine. He switched off the light and leaned back against the tree and fell asleep.

It took Major Ben "Dutch" Ryland twelve days to work his way down from the mountains. His rations gave out after three days. He lived on small animals he killed with the high-velocity folding .22 rifle from his survival kit. He managed fish twice by aiming carefully into shallow streams when the unknown-to-him but apparently edible creatures swam lazily near the surface. He used the water-purification tablets from his survival kit to assure the potability of the liquid he gathered from streams. On the eighth day he lost the rifle while fording a narrow but swift stream; making the crossing with one arm broken and the other trying to hang onto his precious rifle was too much. He also lost the survival kit. Going under, he found the weight of the kit too much for only one arm; it was either dump the load or drown. His last four days were spent without food. The water he drank, without chemical purification, assaulted his stomach and made him feverish. Heat, insects, pain from his broken arm, no food and the debilitating effects of the jungle waters nearly finished him. He survived because he was strong and stubborn and kept his head. He worked his way due south, stumbling through thick growth and over tangled underfooting until he reached the banks of the Sicuani River. Through his fever he recalled that the river ran generally southeast as it dropped from the mountain regions. If that were so he must follow the river. It was worse travel than before because the jungle was thicker and teeming with insects that bit him, puffed up his eyes. He went along the river bank because it assured him he would not wander in circles in trackless undergrowth. One late afternoon he stumbled into the riverside town of Azul, nestled beneath a looming mountain peak. A native doctor kept him alive as he was transported, feverish and ranting, downriver to the larger community of Ayabaca. Directly across the river by a wooden bridge was a large grass airstrip. Once every three days a small plane landed, bringing in mail and supplies. Alive but still feverish, Ryland was carried to the airplane and strapped in and then flown two hundred and ninety miles to the nearest Peruvian Air Force base. Within an hour a United States Air Force medical team was on hand.

The search for the missing C-130E had been abandoned a week before, along with hope for any surviving crewmen. Next morning Ryland was flown from the Peruvian base directly back to the United States, nonstop to the medical facilities of Norton Air Force Base in California, which not coincidentally was the headquarters of the Air Inspector General of the United States Air Force—and site of an unlisted office of JMSIC, Joint Military Services Intelligence Command.

JMSIC had been sent, in code, a summary of the inchoate ramblings of the feverish Major Ryland. There could be no paved road, highway or any other such work of man where Ryland had landed in his parachute. Well, he was delirious. Maybe so, thought a colonel in JMSIC. But he knew Dutch Ryland and had the highest regard for the major's skills and judgment, especially when engineering skills and acumen were involved—even when none of these reported things could

15

be (in the face of all evidence) present where they were allegedly found.

Major Ryland came out of his fever. He was strong, in superior physical shape, and he recovered swiftly. His memory seemed unimpaired. He stuck to his story. The details were stamped MOST SECRET and distributed to a limited number of government agencies. Among that list was OSO—the Office of Special Operations, catch-all of undercover maneuvering. What Ryland had reported was so outlandish that no other agency seemed willing to consider it—to try to find out *what* might be there. *Something* made the major's roadway. It was surely very old. Maybe ancient, fashioned by devices unknown to present-day technology.

In a wooded suburb of Washington, D.C., the JMSIC report stopped at the desk of Oscar Goldman, second from the top in OSO. He read the report. There were too many missing pieces in this thing, which upset Goldman's orderly thought processes. He took his telephone from its cradle, punched in a number. He asked questions, raised his brows at the answers. He replaced the telephone and turned to his dictating machine, spoke for nearly twenty minutes, gave the tape to his secretary to transcribe. He went to the commissary for coffee. By the time he returned, his memo was typed and he'd made a decision.

Minutes later he was meeting with Jackson McKay, the huge man who ran OSO. McKay read out Goldman for bothering him with such drivel. Goldman waited him out and counterattacked. A good exchange. A method they'd used with each other for years. It brought most everything out of the woodwork.

JMSIC had officially requested the services of OSO for the investigation. In the end McKay yielded. "Call him," he said to Goldman.

"He's on a fishing trip. A year overdue, I might add. *You* call him. You're big boss."

"Get out," McKay told him pleasantly. "You're in charge of the dirty work."

Goldman got to his feet. "It won't be easy. I'll lay odds he hasn't got his caller with him."

McKay agreed, but wagered Rudy Wells would be with him and he would have his caller with him. "Use that frequency."

CHAPTER II

THE ROD came back, bending at precisely the right angle, and the wrist snapped forward, bringing the rod whistling in response. Steve Austin watched the fly lure whip neatly along the rocky side of the stream before settling where he had aimed on the far side of a clear, deep pool. He turned to grin at his companion, Dr. Rudy Wells—outfitted in a splendid if somewhat garish ensemble of rubberized boots, bright-orange hunting trousers and a brighter yellow jacket, all topped with an outlandish hat bristling with flies and lures. He also had managed a pepper-and-salt beard. "I suppose you expect me to applaud."

Austin laughed. "You're jealous, Doc. Also clumsy. Come on, let's see how fast you can tangle your line."

"Well, move to the side and let a pro have at it."

Austin moved slowly to the right. He gestured to the pool, where his lure skipped in short dashes across the water. "All those beautiful trout just waiting to leap right into our frying pan." He turned again to study his line. "Make you a deal. First one to score has dinner cooked by the empty-handed."

Wells moved to the edge of the stream, took aim and cast out his line. It went to the side of the pool where Wells had noticed telltale movement just beneath the surface. "A deal." Both men brought in their lines slowly, cast again, and then a third time.

Austin's line snapped taut. "Hey, here comes dinner!"

"Bring him in first," Wells challenged, and a moment later shouted himself, as a second trout struck, boiling water and leaping high before he went under. Each man worked his trout with care, moving his fish slowly toward him, ready to dip a net into the water to land the catch. Wells was in the better position to land his and he stepped several feet into the stream, the net poised. He brought his rod up high, positioning the trout just right and—

A high-pitched electronic whine came from his jacket. A boot slipped on a rock—the net went in one direction, the rod in another, and Dr. Wells in still another, to splash full-length into the stream. The piercing whine continued without letup as he lay sputtering in the water. He raised himself slowly, dripping, to stand wide-legged in water above his knees, and looked quietly at the other man.

Austin's face was a tight mask. He turned his back to the doctor and continued working his catch toward him. Wells made no move, waiting. Austin landed the trout, a beauty, at least five or six pounds, then walked slowly from the stream to their small encampment.

Finally he turned to face Wells. "Can't you turn off that damned thing?"

Wells walked from the stream, shaking his arms. "It doesn't

turn off for ten minutes. You know they need ten minutes for direction finding."

"Hand it here, Rudy."

"There's no off-switch."

"I know that. Just give it to me."

Wells unzipped the inside pocket of his jacket, removed the sealed transceiver. Free of the jacket the sound was louder, more insistent. Wells winced as he handed over the instrument.

For a moment Austin held it, seeming to feel the weight in his hand. Suddenly the fingers closed, steel pincers squeezing.

"Steve, don't do—" Wells cut off his own warning as useless. Austin ground it in his bionics hand and threw it away.

Wells looked at him. "We can't just ignore the call." He didn't have to say the rest, that the electronic signal was used only by OSO in an emergency. The signal didn't provide for response with the compact transceiver. It received its radio trigger no matter where its geographic location; the signal was sent from the system of military communications satellites in high orbit. It was *always* received. When the comsat signal triggered the deliberately provoking shriek, it also activated a transmitter in the device. The unheard radio signal that flashed back could provide highly accurate triangulation to locate the man carrying the device. The man with this signal equipment was supposed to get to the nearest telephone and call in to a secret number at OSO. Steve Austin obviously was in no hurry to respond to the emergency transmission.

"Steve," Rudy Wells began again. "I said we can't just ignore—"

"Watch me, Doc. Watch me do the greatest job of ignoring you ever saw. Look, I haven't had a break for more than a year. Same for you. Every chance we get to move out from under is fouled up by someone yelling emergency. I came here to fish. I am going to fish." He gestured to the trout still in the net. "And that's your job right now. Remember? The bet?"

Wells nodded and set up the fish for cleaning. A banked fire and glowing coals had already been prepared. He decided not to press the issue with Steve. He really couldn't blame the man. Three times in the last year he'd gone out for OSO.

The first had been an underwater expedition off the coast of Venezuela using android porpoises, during which Steve had worked his way deep into a Russian submarine cave and had nearly paid with his life for the pictures he'd brought out within his eyesocket camera. He's been depthcharged, attacked by divers with knives, and shot. He'd made it back with even *his* overwhelming strength nearly depleted and his bionics systems riddled and failing. Electronic "superman" or not, there were definite nonsuper, very human limits.

No sooner had he been patched up than McKay at OSO was pushing him back into action. They used Steve for assignments that were likely to be beyond most ordinary men. A brilliant mind, the build of an athlete combined with the bionics systems that made Steve Austin a cybernetics organism. *Cyborg.* Funny, the way they'd come to accept Steve in that role ... he was so very human and vulnerable in so many respects.

There had been relatively conventional years as a test pilot, including three ejections from crippled, burning aircraft. Then openings in the space program and NASA had snapped up his application. Along with his experience and six thousand hours in the air went a master's degree in geology, another in aeronautical engineering and still another in, of all things, history and cultural studies. After commanding the last Apollo mission to the moon, Steve turned down the Skylab program and came back to the sprawling flight-test center in the California desert.

The Shuttle program was *the* program for the future. Nearly everything that would go into space, manned or robot, would

22

make the trip aboard the delta-winged Shuttle emerging from the drawing boards. There'd be a NASA Shuttle and also an Air Force edition, and Steve Austin wanted in on the ground floor. The Shuttle needed its principles tested in smaller forerunners known as lifting bodies; "flying bathtubs" to those on the projects. Wicked, given to sudden violent rolls to the right or the left, they were intended to breach the barrier reefs in the sky, get the flight and design problems solved so that the future Shuttle could fly in comfort and safety.

Steve became chief project officer as well as chief test pilot with the M3F5. A B-52 dropped him at 45,000 feet. As he fell away, Steve ignited the rocket chambers in the belly of his flying bathtub. He took her up to 120,000 feet and sailed through a swooping curve from near-vacuum. As he began to bring her out of the high-speed glide she began her crazy rolling motion that was at the heart of the test—to find out what maneuvers by the pilot could damp the oscillations. He held her beautifully until he flared. He had it done, inches from touching down on the hard desert floor. She rolled, snapped to the left. Silver metal thundered across the desert in a flaming, disintegrating shambles, with Steve Austin trapped inside, being mangled by the forces of the tumbling crash. In that long moment until the wreckage came to a smouldering stop, Steve Austin "died."

He had been a brilliant test pilot, an astronaut, a warm human being of high intelligence and diverse skills. When the crash crews arrived at the metal wreckage, Rudy Wells with them, that Steve Austin was gone. Crushed, broken, unconscious, he was rushed to the emergency medical facility at Edwards Air Force Base, and to the skill of its Air Force flight surgeons. But only one of those men, a physician and close friend named Rudy Wells, could penetrate through and beyond the medical procedures to keep alive what they had dragged from the wreckage. *If* they could keep him alive.

Both legs amputated. The left arm mangled so badly it had been torn from the body in the crash. Ribs shattered, jaw smashed; all to be replaced in a long, tedious and demanding process with metal alloys and ceramics and plastics. The heart had been damaged but it would heal. Not so a main artery and its valve, but in spectacular open-heart surgery the damaged parts were removed and a Hufnagel valve implanted. His left eye was blind. They might replace it with an infrared detector or even a camera, but he would be at least partially blind until they perfected an artificial eye. They were working on it. . . .

Ashburn and Killian were the two surgeons who had performed the near-miraculous work—attended to the skull fracture, concussion, burned skin, lung damage. Dr. Rudy Wells assisted, but he was essential to keep alive not the body but the mind and spirit of Steve Austin. For a while Steve hated him. Steve felt he had become a basket case—one arm and one eye hardly qualified him for the human race. But he survived, precariously, against his mind and will that asked for death. He'd been kept unconscious for weeks. Time, the new healer. Time for shock to ebb slowly from the remaining body and from the mind. Time for the trillions of cells to reform, adapt.

The Air Force flew him to their new bionics laboratory carved into the flanks of the Colorado Rockies. The lab was engineering and life sciences and biology and cybernetics and surgery and experimentation. Advanced computers held equal place with the skill of human surgeons, for the computer could reproduce the mechanical-electrical equivalent of every element of construction and function of, for example in the case of Steve, the human arm and hand and leg.

The computer digested what it learned, but was taxed to reduce to intelligible, functional symbols the handiwork of nature. Symbols became numbers, numbers became digits with special meaning to waiting doctors, scientists, technicians and engineers. In those mathematical symbols was the lodestone, blueprints for creating a living simulation of what had been a human arm, leg, elbow, rib, knee or finger.

Some argued the semantics of *living,* or *life.* The human body is no mere mechanical instrument. It does function, though, on messages generated by electrochemical reaction. Nervous energy is electrical energy, even if the intricacy of the human structure calls for a better analogy than an internally powered, mobile battery case.

Bionics did not contest the semantics. Nor did it seek agreement. The calling of these surgeons under the direction of Dr. Michael Killian was the work itself. The results. Bionics. *Bios* from the Greek for life; *ics,* "in the manner after." A bionics limb was a recreation of the living member. Steve Austin—cyborg—would be the beneficiary of cybernetic computer technology achieving bionic simulation of nature.

When they finished repairing his heart they turned to his crushed skull. They replaced the bone with cesium and, where needed, new alloys. They designed a spongy center layer and another outer layer to protect the brain case inside. As a result he could endure a direct blow far greater than the sledge-hammer shocks that cracked his skull in the first place. The ribs, cracked and splintered, were replaced with flexible metal and wired to the musculature, as nature had originally done, to keep them in place, flexing when needed, providing a protective cage when needed.

None of this could compare with the wonder of recreated limbs—to the arm with its elbow and its bionics bones and cartilage and the dexterity of wrist and fingers and opposed digit, as well as to the legs with their computer-directed systems.

It was one thing to construct the limbs that were to receive the nerve impulses flowing to and from the brain, nerve impulses that were literally electrical signals. It was another to mimic the nerve fibers, the systems for transmitting the impulses from the brain into the spinal cord and on down to the message networks. To Steve's arm stump they double-engaged the bionics and the natural bone to exceed by multiples the original levels of strength and resistance. They connected the severed nerves and muscles with bionics nerves and muscles. The two systems were compatible. The signals came through but were too weak for the bionics system. Science could duplicate the living limb but it could not make it work on the whisper of current sufficient for the natural limb. So within the bionics arm and legs went miniaturized nuclear-powered generators that spun silently at speeds measured in thousands of revolutions per second.

A signal flashed from Steve's brain until it reached the part of him that was living because of computer and machine lathe. The signal entered the bionics system, was sensed and flashed to an amplifier within that system. Now it was retransmitted with a current many times stronger than when received. The small nuclear generators fed power through the man-made duplications of nature's pulleys and cables, which twisted, pulled, bent, contracted, squeezed. But artificial fingertips lacked sensitivity. A cybernetic hand with no more effort than was needed to pulp a rose could do the same to human bone. The need was for discretionary feel, which was achieved through vibrating pads, sensors, amplifiers and feedback. Now the steel-boned hand that with a single transmitted impulse could crush and kill could also caress a woman's skin.

For month after month Steve Austin, reborn as cyborg, sought to create a physical and emotional knowledge and acceptance of himself. For months he stumbled and fell, weaved and swayed. His systems shorted and jerked spasmodically; he was clumsy, felt himself a bumbling fool, was filled with the rage of frustration. Finally, thanks especially to the dedication of Dr. Wells, his technicians, and a giant of a man, Marty Schiller, who walked on two artificial legs of his own, Steve made it and discovered there even were compensations.

If the bionics arm and legs were not quite the same as the original limbs, they were in some ways superior. Steve's arm was more than the ordinary natural one. It functioned, if needed, as a battering ram, a vise, a bludgeon—a tool and a weapon. His legs had the potentiality of driving pistons. His heart, respiration and circulatory systems benefited from the need to serve a body with two legs and one arm less than before. The bionics systems with their nuclear amplifiers attended to energy needs so that Steve's potential endurance increased. He was, however, as dependent as ever on his heart and lungs and brain and other unaffected systems.

But what of the psychology of a man who has, for example, suffered impotence—not through genital injury or damage to the nerve network splicing the spinal column but through fear that no woman could feel anything for a half-man, half-machine. And even that had been overcome, through the superior medicine of a loving woman.

For all this Steve had a price to pay. To OSO in the person of Oscar Goldman, right hand and alter-ego to Jackson McKay, its director. Goldman was five feet, five inches tall. Somewhere in his past he had been a special-agent paratrooper and ranger. He was skilled in weapons. He was also more than passing shrewd in sizing up people, in recruiting even the reluctant for the Office of Special Operations. He could correlate an enormous quantity of fact from various disciplines. He knew how to put on the squeeze.

He had begun with Rudy Wells, which was when the project to create a cyborg was born. Goldman saw in Steve Austin the promise of a most extraordinary special agent. The Air Force would do everything to make a new life for Steve, but that "everything" had limits. Artificial legs and an arm. A glass eye. Patch and mend and bandage. Some psychiatric treatment. They'd release a man who would doubtless take the first opportunity to finish the job they'd interrupted when they dragged his remains from the wreckage on the California desert.

Oscar Goldman had promised more. He had come prepared to invest six million dollars, the sum authorized by Jackson McKay. Sympathy? Feeling? None of these, Goldman told Rudy Wells, was to be measured against the offer. Steve Austin would be an experiment. He was more than the torn remains of a man. He had been a man with brilliance and training and knowledge at his command. It could all be brought to life again. And more.

OSO would pay for the surgery and the bionics development. They would pay for the facilities and the personnel that would be needed to train this new man. And when it was done, they would present their bill.

To pay it Steve Austin would be obliged to train and perform as a special agent for OSO. Wherever, whatever, whenever. That was the deal, and Rudy Wells had accepted because he had no choice and Goldman knew it.

Steve's new body made parts of him potentially killing mechanisms in themselves. With special devices and weaponry integrated with his bionics systems Austin was capable of certain missions on his own that even a company of men could not accomplish.

OSO proceeded to exact payment from this man, this cyborg. First the mission into the Soviet submarine caverns on the coast of South America. Next a mission into Egypt against Soviet-sponsored Arab extremists, for which he needed his skills as a pilot plus the endurance of the cyborg. A shadow remained from that time; Steve had teamed with a girl he knew only as Tamara, an Israeli special agent, lovely, courageous and intelligent, fired with life. He crossed the treacherous Sinai with an unconscious Tamara lashed to his back. His pistonlike legs carried him and his burden across scorching wastes. He survived once again—but more dead than alive.

Recuperation took months, but Steve had not forgotten her. He returned to Israel—three days after Tamara had been killed in a border fight. A friend took him to her grave and he stood there alone, trying to cry. The grief went too deep.

He returned to the States, met by his closest friend. Rudy Wells flew back with Steve to Colorado. More training. New devices and systems to be tested. Drown the grief in challenge. They were near the end of that special program when Jackson McKay sent out the word for Steve to report to OSO headquarters and for months afterward Steve was involved in a double life. After an elaborately stage-managed incident he fled the United States as a fugitive, compounding one felony with another when he and his buddy Marty Schiller stole a Boeing 707 from its maintenance facility and disappeared across the Atlantic, finally to land in Libya. It was an act calculated to bring Steve to the attention of—and able to infiltrate—an organization dealing in the theft, sale and even use of nuclear weapons. In the long months that followed, as he played out his assigned role, he became—though unintentionally—associated with a nuclear blast that took the life of his friend Marty Schiller, and *that* was to stay a very long time with Steve. Little matter that he had been powerless to prevent it, or that his mission had "succeeded." He still felt he had blood to wash from his hands, an agony to wash out of his mind.

There had been more repairs to his system. Rudy Wells worried that Steve might be turning too deeply into himself, and it was with enormous relief that he heard Steve propose the fishing trip up in Wyoming. A cyborg could be repaired. The man Steve Austin had to heal himself.

Now, at the end of only their first day at the stream, that

electronic signal had gone off. Thinking of it all, Rudy Wells decided Steve was right when he'd crushed the transceiver in his bionics hand. Let them find *us*.

He got to his feet. "If you can move that tin butt of yours over here," he said to Steve, "you can have the greatest trout ever cooked by man."

That night, in his sleeping bag underneath the stars, Rudy Wells glanced at Steve already fast asleep and raised the image in his mind of his extraordinary friend: Ex-fighter pilot, former astronaut, six feet one, flat-bellied, lean-muscled. Blue eyes. Check that—one blue eye, natural; one blue eye, plastic. And the dark brown hair had grown on someone else before implantation into the steel shell surrounding Steve's skull. He looked a lean 180 pounds. With his bionics systems he weighed 240. He carried it with ease. Not at first, but now he did because he'd managed to integrate himself. He was, his friend decided, a very human success. And he was entitled. To hell with them all. We came here to fish. . . .

In the morning the helicopter found them over their breakfast fire.

CHAPTER III

OSCAR GOLDMAN looked down at the figures in the small clearing, turned to the pilot and pointed. "Can you take us down there?"

"No way, Mr. Goldman. We'd never get the rotors within those trees."

"Well, take us a bit lower then."

The downwash from the powerful turbine Alouette sent the coffeepot flying over on its side, tumbled camp supplies, sprayed the men with gravel.

Goldman saw Austin bending down. "Get us out of here *quick,*" he told the pilot.

A rock smashed into the plexiglass bubble and ricocheted away. Goldman saw Steve Austin taking aim. The bionics arm was a near blur of movement as Goldman ducked away from the open door. The second rock thrown with near-bullet force banged off the belly of the helicopter. The pilot needed no further convincing. The turbine howled as he went to full power for altitude and distance.

Goldman pointed. "That clearing over there will do. Let me off there and then get this thing away. It's eight-thirty. I want you back here at noon, understand?"

The pilot shook his head as he circled into the wind for the landing. Goldman unstrapped his belt and started from the machine as it rocked gently to the surface. "Just add any damage to the bill. Noon, remember?" He half-turned as he crouched beneath the whirling blades over his head, then moved quickly away, not even looking back as the sudden roar of power and whistling rotors told him the pilot was on his way.

He walked along the edge of the stream to the small camp. Austin and Wells stared at him. Goldman smiled. "Nothing like a warm welcome."

Austin turned to the doctor.

"What's the penalty if I kill this character?"

"They make you fill out forms. In quadruplicate."

"He's not worth it."

Steve accepted the cup offered by Wells, who hesitated a moment before handing one to Goldman. He filled a third cup for himself and sat cross-legged on the ground. "All right, Oscar, let's have the bad news."

Goldman took a pull at the coffee, placed the cup on the log beside him. "We have a trip for you."

"I'm *on* a trip," Steve said.

"This one has higher priority."

"Not interested."

"You will be, in fact, you'll both be interested." He turned to the doctor. "You're going with him."

"How do I fit in? And where are we supposed to go?"

"Peru. The high Andes. An area close to the Cordillera Vilcabamba."

"I know of it," the doctor said. "What are you after, Oscar?"

Goldman finished his coffee. "We're not sure. The Cordillera Vilcabamba, the maps say, is a high and level plain in the Peruvian Andes. About ten or twelve thousand feet high. But the maps are wrong. We found out only recently just how wrong. The Vilcabamba is a treacherous mountain range. Naked rock. Up to fourteen thousand feet or more. That's just the general idea. The Vilcabamba is in southeastern Peru. You can better identify our area of concern by El Misti. That's a volcano, still smoking, exactly 23,482 feet high. The volcano—I'm using straight-line distance—is some forty miles from the native town of Azul. About thirty miles downriver—that's the Sicuani and it covers a lot of jungle—there's a larger town. Ayabaca. It has a grass airstrip, apparently a good one about four thousand feet long."

Steve said, "How far from Lima?"

"Three hundred and twenty miles straight east, give or take twenty. The area we're interested in lies due south, off the bottom flank of the Vilcabamba."

"You said the maps were all wrong for that area."

Goldman nodded. "They are. That's why we've made you our own charts. The best we could get from the ERTS satellite and Skylab. Also, anything that might have turned up from the Gemini and Apollo flights that crossed over the area."

"No aerial photographs?"

"Very few. In fact, we were working with the Peruvian government on a special effort to get some mapping photography. We were running a C-130 up and down the range to get full spectrum—visible light, radar topography, infrared."

"And?"

"Mostly bad luck. The winds that come down the slopes of El Misti are wild. There's also a peculiar sort of inversion layer

33

that creates a great deal of fog or mist, not to mention the cloud cover."

Steve poured a second cup of coffee, did the same for Wells. Goldman declined. "I gather," Steve said, "that the net of all this effort isn't much."

Goldman agreed. "But what we don't have, you can fill in when you're there."

"Which brings us to the why of your unwelcome visit," Wells said.

Goldman thought. "The why is rather hazy. There's something there, way high up, that shouldn't be there. We'd like to know about it. During the last mission flown in the area of Cordillera Vilcabamba we lost the C-130E aircraft assigned to the mapping program." He saw Steve's attention sharpen. "It was at night. We're reasonably sure about what happened. The aircraft was caught in what are apparently swift-forming and unusually powerful thunderstorms. Since there's no meteorological service anywhere in that area, night flying is a hit-or-miss operation. This particular machine got caught in one of the more severe buildups, maybe in an entire squall line. At least that seemed to be the situation as we could best determine it from the one survivor. The airplane was hit with something that seemed to be lightning. It—"

"Hold on, you can hardly mistake a lightning strike, Oscar."

"Yes you can, Steve. It could have been lightning. Or a severe electrical short in the aircraft system that ignited kerosene fumes released by the drastic bending motions of the wing during the storm. Or an engine explosion. Or a heat ray or—"

"A *what?*"

Goldman turned to Wells. "I said a heat ray, doctor. Or maybe a plasma bolt. Or a laser beam. Any one of them *could* be mistaken for lightning. There seems little doubt, though, that the airplane was destroyed by lightning. Major Ben

34

Ryland, Dutch Ryland, was the only survivor. His report strongly supports this. And the nature of his body burns, the way he was blown clear of the exploding aircraft—"

"What happened to Ryland?" Steve asked.

"Hit in a wind he estimated at thirty to forty knots. He went into the top of a tree. The impact broke his left arm. He fell through and just before he hit the ground the canopy snagged in the trees. He dropped the last bit without too much difficulty. It was raining hard. He had his survival kit. He set a splint, took rations and morphine, used his mylar blanket for warmth and cover. Next morning he decided to check out something he had seen by flasher during the night. Ryland wisely didn't trust his own memory of the night. He'd been in shock, had jumped, had broken his arm. Where he came down was almost unbroken tree cover, so aerial or satellite photography would show only treetops and the heavy growth. Also the area due south of the flank of Cordillera Vilcabamba where Ryland landed, at least by any records we or the Peruvians have, has never been explored. It's so wild and unknown that even the mountains—and they're rough—are shown on maps as a generally flat plateau. There has never been the slightest evidence that the area was ever occupied, not recently and not even in ancient times. We checked this out with Peruvian archeologists and—"

"Get to it, Oscar," Steve said.

"Major Ryland found a highway running through the jungle."

"Highway?" Wells echoed.

"Highway. Not some rutted path. Not something for animals. Not something pounded into the ground. I mean a *highway* made of stone blocks. How deep or heavy, Ryland couldn't tell. Their pattern was jumbled, no geometric design. No careful setting of one block after another. It was Ryland's opinion that the area had had rock of different sizes pounded into an approximate shape and then some kind of cutting tool was used to make the roadway absolutely level. *Absolutely level.* Ryland made a point of that. He said the surface, accounting for weathering, mossy growth and the like, was almost as smooth as polished marble."

"Did Ryland have any idea how long this ... highway extended?"

"No. And with his broken arm he wasn't in the mood for sightseeing, even if what he saw was impossible. He also had to walk his way out. He guessed, and he was right, that the odds on being found by air search were next to zero. So he walked along the highway to a point where he saw the best chance for working down from the mountains. He headed downslope and into the jungle. It took him twelve days to make it to the outpost town of Azul. He was nearly dead when the natives brought him downriver to the airstrip at Ayabaca. He estimated he'd walked the highway three or four miles. Now, before he started, as far as he could see to the north, the highway just went on and on. He walked, let's say, for those four miles to the south. Before he turned off and started down toward the valley he said the road stretched out of sight."

"Did he say anything else?" Steve asked.

"Yes. That he could find no signs of wear from a wheeled or other type of vehicle on the highway."

"I'm not wholly surprised," Rudy Wells said as the other two looked at him. "I've heard of such road systems in South America, mostly in Peru but some in Bolivia. As I suspect you know, Oscar, I've been interested in this for some time. We've heard of such roadways made up of huge blocks cut with amazing geometric precision. They apparently were brought together up to great heights by means still unknown. In Bolivia, near Santa Cruz, long stretches of what appear to be stone have been reported to be *concrete* ... a strange sort of roadway in some places twenty feet wide, in others thirty, with joined diamond shapes running the length of the road that had been broken up in some places by earthquake or flood or some kind of volcanic activity. That roadway is made of concrete, yet concrete didn't come into general use for thousands of years *after* it's estimated the roadway was built."

Steve looked at his friend. "This is getting to sound like that business about ancient astronauts, chariots of the gods and—"

"Erich von Daniken," Wells offered. "Much of what he writes about, when you read between his conclusions, is hard fact—things that have so far not been explained, like that highway in Bolivia. He's accumulated a great deal of material. Say with the skeptics that at best only a small percentage amounts to hard fact. Forget his suppositions and rather special interpretations of the Bible and other historical works. Forget *all* that. What do you do about the percentage of fact? What can you do with everything else that is a complete mystery?"

"Like what?" Steve asked. "It's one thing to talk about ancient mysteries, but how do you draw sensible conclusions about them?"

Oscar Goldman was pleased. He had, as Wells thought, known about the doctor's interest and active studies in this field. As long as the doctor held his friend Steve Austin's interest, he'd be doing the job of convincing that he, Goldman, had come here to do.

"Well, for starters," Wells began, "there's the ancient city of Nazca. It's in the Palpa Valley in Peru, close to the sea and adjacent to the flanks of the Andes. . . . I never thought of this before but there's another ancient city roughly in the area . . . I'm talking about Cuzco that lies on the southeastern edge of the Cordillera Vilcabamba that's—"

"In the same area," Steve broke in, "where that C-130 went down. Any connection to it?"

"Hard to say. They *were* in a storm and—"

"Never mind, Rudy, go on."

"Well, the Palpa Valley has a strip of level ground a bit more than a mile wide and nearly forty miles long. There's some strange stuff on the ground. It seems to be stone but it resembles rusted iron. No one is really sure what it is. But that's not the real point. I once flew over this plain, Nazca, and I tell you it's a shaky experience. The whole plain has enormous lines that follow a geometric pattern. There's no reason for the pattern. There are large areas that are trapezoids. Some of the lines run in parallel, others intersect. But they *are* geometric and they are real and . . . well, they're there."

"Any ideas?" Steve said.

"The archeologists tend to suggest a system of roads built by the Incas."

"You agree?"

"It seems to me to raise more questions than it answers. If they are roads, why do they run parallel for long distances? And the roads end abruptly. Why? There hasn't been any natural disruption of the surface features—lava flows or quakes. The end of the roads, to use that name for the moment, is too sudden."

"How about disease, invasion, change of power among their priests?"

Wells agreed readily. "Another possibility is that they form some important element in a religion we still can't figure out. There are theories that the lines represent a link to astronomy. Someone else talks about a calendar. Von Daniken says that when he flew over the plain at Nazca he could make out the geometric pattern of an airfield for visitors from space."

"What?"

"I'm telling you what Von Daniken said."

"You seem an instant disbeliever," Oscar Goldman said.

"It doesn't take much," Steve answered. "First, anyone who's capable of flight through interplanetary space doesn't

38

need a runway thirty or forty miles long. If you needed that to stop you'd be using a winged vehicle that would be coming down so fast it'd be tearing itself to pieces with heat. We can take heat in the upper atmosphere on re-entry because the air is so thin. But down here? The shock waves would be incredible. The speed of touchdown would make the slightest bounce a blow that would tear apart any machine. Does this man offer any other explanation?"

"He does," Wells said. "He suggests that an airborne machine somehow managed to communicate instructive intimations to the local residents. They responded without knowing why—to some deep inner hunch, you might call it. And when they were finished, this was to be their signpost to the gods that they were worthy of being visited by godlike creatures."

"But you can't," Steve said, "label your own conclusions as fact just because nobody knows the answer to a mystery and therefore can't say for *sure* you're wrong. This reminds me of people who ask me if I believe in UFOs. I say, no, I don't. They get sore and want to know if I don't believe in life on other planets. No connection between question-answer and conclusion. Same thing goes for whether or not I believe in astronauts visiting earth ages ago. Maybe they did. I just say there's never been evidence that stands up to a real test."

"And the major's highway in Peru, and the one in Bolivia that shouldn't be there?" Goldman said.

"So there are highways. And they're mysterious. And we can't understand how they got there. But because they're there, and we can't figure out how come, doesn't prove that beings came into this solar system and built the things. There's an old saying that countless scientific experiments prove conclusively that the beating of tom-toms always causes the sun to reappear after an eclipse."

"We have another one in our trade," Rudy said. "It's about

a doctor who decided he needed a hobby to get his mind off all the ills of his patients. So he took up training a flea to respond to his verbal command. He did pretty well. The flea, among other things, would jump when he got the command to jump. After a while the doctor got tired of the sport and decided to turn his hobby into a scientific experiment. He pulled the two front legs off the flea and said, 'jump.' And the flea jumped. Then he pulled off the two center legs and said 'jump.' Again the flea jumped. Then he pulled off the last pair of legs and commanded the flea to jump. It didn't jump. He shouted and threatened the flea, but it still wouldn't jump. The doctor then wrote a scientific thesis to prove that when you remove all six legs from a flea, it loses its sense of hearing."

Goldman indulged in a smile. "I'll steal that for McKay."

"Let me take it a bit further," Steve said. "Rudy, aren't there some unusual astronomical records that come from the Incas, or Aztecs and Mayans?"

"No question, Steve. One of the best known is the so-called Great Idol of Tiahuanaco, a block of stone that weighs about twenty tons and is marked with precision-made symbols. There's argument about how to interpret these symbols, but one holds that the symbols actually represent an extraordinary collection of astronomical data. All of it's based on recognition of the earth being a sphere, and the block seems to go back far past the point when a round earth first came into scientific favor. Some authorities claim the stone block is around twenty-seven thousand years old."

"And the opposition?"

"They don't agree about astronomical knowledge being involved. They say no one has yet deciphered or translated the markings. And as for the age of the stone, you can get five experts in one room and each will give you a different answer.

"Let's say there are more of these astronomical records. Let's say they're accurate. I've read the Mayans had some kind of observatories and did some remarkable work in astronomy, and that their calendar was very accurate. We know about great European astronomers from history. We call some of them geniuses, but I've never heard anyone say the same about the Mayans and other Central and South American groups who may also have had geniuses in their religious leaders that spent lifetimes in this kind of research."

"You know," Steve added, "we should all have learned from the moon. Never trust conclusive evidence either pro or con until we wrap up the details. How many thousands of years have people studied the moon? How many millions of pictures were taken by observatories around the world? There was an amazing similarity to the pattern. The moon was filled with jagged peaks and crags, sharp rocks and God knows what else. An astronaut would risk tearing or puncturing his suit from rocks if he even brushed against them. Except the moon had been shaved, ground and powdered. The mountains were round and gentle. No one's ever seen a sharp or a jagged peak anywhere on the moon. Every astronomer and scientist in the world misinterpreted the photographs. They saw jagged *shadows* so they figured the mountains must be jagged.

"And what about Mars. They said it was everything from a long-dead civilization to a flourishing one that had built a planet-girdling network of canals. We could see flashes of light on Mars at different times and people spoke seriously about hydrogen-bomb explosions. The waves of darkening were vegetation, and so on.

"Well, I was pretty involved in assessing what we learned about Mars because we've had it as a program target a long time. Mariner Four took pictures that covered about 1 percent of the planet. We saw craters and right away the old theories went out the window. Mars was cratered like the moon; Mars was like the moon. So we fired up Mariners Six and Seven, and they took pictures of 20 percent of the surface. They saw

41

not only the craters but also featureless terrain and chaotic terrain of jumbled faults and the icecaps. The pictures made it clear Mars had been dead a long time. No signs of life. No signs of any growth. No signs of water or oxygen or anything else. A dead world.

"The conclusions were based on hard scientific evidence and they were wrong. We put Mariner Nine into Mars' orbit. It photographed the whole planet. We all wondered how we could have been so wrong. Mars was anything but dead, it was dynamic. It had volcanoes that were—that are—pouring hundreds of millions of gallons of water in gaseous form into its atmosphere every day. There's a place on Mars called Nix Olympica, one of the so-called mysterious features that's always been described as bright-ringed. They got some good shots from a couple of thousand miles out with Mariners Six and Seven. No doubt at all about the bright ring. Then Mariner Nine got some close-ups of this bright ring. Know what it turned out to be?"

Rudy Wells spoke up. "A volcano that was about fifty thousand feet high and bigger than the whole state of Missouri."

"Right. They also found a canyon, like the Grand Canyon, that stretched along the Martian equator. Three thousand miles long, seventy or eighty miles wide and four miles deep. And evidence of running water in the past. And proof the icecaps had water instead of just carbon dioxide in them ... it's a long list. Point is that even when we've had hard scientific observation and apparent proof, we've ended up with the yellow stuff all over our faces. Which also means, Oscar, that I don't buy fast conclusions either way, including the validity of suppositions such as Mr. von Däniken's."

Goldman stood and stretched. "All of which, Steve, only confirms that you're the man for this job. And Rudy, because of his own studies and special interest in the field, and because he's a doctor."

"I still don't see why it's so important for me to make this trip," Steve said.

"Powers of observation, for one thing. You're a trained geologist. You know what to look for. You don't, as you've just indicated, draw hasty conclusions. You reject unsupported answers as nothing more than speculation. Yet you have an open mind. We believe this roadway reported by Major Ryland also has potential for getting a lead to something else. Optics. Incredible development of optics by a race that's been lost for unknown thousands of years. They're referred to as the Caya. You won't find references to them in books of the scientific establishment, but they are supposed to have come from the same area where Ryland found that road."

"Then send Ryland back. He's the one with actual experience in the area."

"But he lacks *your* experience," Goldman said. "You've commanded an expedition to the moon. You're a fine engineer. And you have your, well, built-in advantages that I hardly need to detail. They could be rather vital in the event of any trouble."

"Such as?"

"Well . . . someone—we don't know who—doesn't want us to go back there. Apparently when they brought Ryland down that river to Ayabaca, to the airstrip, he was feverish. He talked about what he'd seen. No one knew anything about such a road and there didn't seem to be any interest. But we've now confirmed that there is very strong interest, that somebody else is looking for what we're trying to find . . . the trail to optics development of so long ago. And perhaps the key to the remarkable energy source that created these mysterious roadways and moved the blocks to such heights.

43

"I had a meeting set up for you two and Ryland for this Thursday. He's been in the base hospital at Norton since he came back here."

"Well, what happened?" Rudy Wells asked. "You talk as if he's not there anymore."

"He's not. Two nights ago someone worked his way into the base hospital, got into Ryland's room, and shot him four times through the head."

CHAPTER IV

THEY CALLED it The Annex. Over the first range of peaks to the west of the Bionics Laboratory that nestled on the eastern slope of the Rockies, due north of the Air Force Academy. The Annex was new to the laboratory, and had been built for the specific purpose of developing and testing different weapons and systems for one man. Steve Austin. Cyborg.

Oscar Goldman had arranged for a Grumman Gulfstream II to be waiting at Jackson Hole Airport in Wyoming. They left the chartered helicopter, boarded the jet and were handed off with top priority from one air-traffic-control center to the next. They were only on the ground one hour before Steve and Dr. Wells were in the modification center of the Bionics Laboratory.

"We're going to load you," Goldman told Steve. "When

you finish in here, call me and we'll meet at the Annex. I want you to try out your new devices as soon as possible. Tomorrow morning you'll meet the three who are going with you."

It was strange for Steve to work on the weapons that would be incorporated within his bionics systems without Marty Schiller. The huge yet gentle man had been . . . Steve forced from his mind the sudden picture of a nuclear fireball swelling over ocean waters, knowing that inside that vaporizing hell was his friend. Stick to now, he told himself.

Jim DiMartino was his new boy. He knew Jim, but not well. He'd worked·for the CIA, was one of the first in the paratrooper strike team of the Air Force before being recruited by Goldman for OSO weapons specialization. DiMartino came into the modification center only minutes after Steve and Rudy Wells had entered the classified area.

His approach was straightforward.

"I don't know much about your mission, Colonel. I get specs and fit them." He walked across the center as he spoke, unlocking a wide cabinet, and returned with three deer rifles. DiMartino gave them each a rifle and held one for demonstration.

"I understand your trip goes under civilian classification, strictly nonmilitary. I don't know where you're going, but it means no military hardware. However, you're not expected to go without rifles—the area, wherever it is, has everything from fourteen-foot snakes to alligators or cayman, to puma and jaguar. Also wild boar, chance of wild dogs. Maybe some unfriendly natives."

"What's been done to these?"

"They've been modified. Most deer rifles of this sort hold six to eight rounds in a clip. You'll have two each of those." He pulled a long clip from his back pocket. "You'll also have a couple of these for each piece. Thirty-six rounds of thirty-thirty and if you press right here"—he demonstrated the release—"this piece is full-automatic. Remember the old M2 carbine? This is three times as effective. When you're around some trouble the suggestion is to insert the small clip and keep the piece on semiauto. The muzzle velocity also is greater than even a deer rifle's. This baby spits."

Steve reached out for the long clip, slammed it in, armed the rifle; his finger stabbed the hidden release and in one motion he spun around and fired. Slugs ripped into the dummies on the far side of the room. Four hammering bursts, the clip was empty, three dummies were cut almost in two. Steve nodded to DiMartino. "Smokeless ammo."

"Yes, sir."

"What's that extra band by the muzzle?"

"Silencer attachment."

DiMartino started bringing out the arsenal. Personal knives cut to Bowie size, only half the weight but twice the strength and with superior balance. Special machetes, lighter than usual, sharp as razors, that wouldn't chip at the weak point of the blade thanks to a carboloy alloy. He went through the mixed supplies—equipment and weapons. Every man to pack one of the new long-barreled, lightweight .38 revolvers developed for the Air Force but also manufactured with no identifying military marks. Couldn't always have a rifle around, but one could strap on a .38 with hip or shoulder holster and get to it quickly with a spring-loaded release. The ammunition for the hand guns ran the gamut from standard issue to explosive rounds and long-burning tracers. Also: thin, strong rope, medical kits, water-purification kits, survival manuals, radio equipment—redundancy in everything. Even a fold-down personal crossbow that attracted Rudy Wells. He stunned DiMartino and Steve when he dropped in six metal bolts and snapped out the bolts almost as fast as a man could fire a semiauto rifle by repeatedly squeezing the trigger. "Where," Steve asked, "did you learn to do *that?*"

"Long time ago, against certain game, especially varmints, I figured it was time to give the opposition a break." Wells patted the crossbow. "You can run out of bolts and you're still in good shape. With that Bowie knife and some string I can make bolts from just about anything that grows in a forest."

"You're hired, personal bodyguard," Steve told him.

Wells then asked DiMartino for a couple of telephoto scopes ... "for obvious reasons and because I can start a fire with one of them. A regular Boy Scout, that's me."

DiMartino told him that, as soon as they finished, "I'm to take you into the medical lab. Everything should be ready for you by then. Shots, I mean. Mr. Goldman wants everybody who's going to get theirs tonight."

"They'll be asleep," Wells reminded him.

"Goldman says to roist them out of bed no matter what time it is. I'll take you to their rooms when you're ready."

"What a way to introduce myself."

After performing his unpopular duty, Rudy Wells went off to find Steve in the bionics lab. He wasn't surprised to see Oscar Goldman hovering over the elaborate chair in which Steve rested while Art Fanier, bionics systems expert who had been on the Cyborg project from its beginning, was carefully unscrewing Steve's left eye. With all he had seen and shared with Steve Austin since that terrible crash in the California desert, with all his experience as a flight surgeon, he still found it unnerving to watch this man yield up parts and pieces of his body.

He moved closer to the chair, to see more clearly and to listen to Goldman's conversation. "One of your group will be equipped with a number of cameras. Normally that would be enough to cover us. Not now, not after what happened to Ryland. We've got to anticipate something not so different occurring again. Which means, Steve, if you find something of significance to photograph, I want you to use the eye-camera. That way, so long as at least *you* get back, we'll have something of what we went after."

Silence as the implications of Goldman's words were absorbed. Then Fanier leaned forward with a small suction disk in his right hand. He steadied his arm against the chair. He hesitated a moment. "Can you keep your eyelid back?" he asked Steve. "I can use the clamps if—"

"Keep going."

Fanier placed the end of the suction disk against the lens of the refractory ceramic eyeball that filled the left eye socket. When he judged the pressure to be exact against the lens, he rotated the disk handle in his fingers. To the left. Goldman and Wells watched intently as the lens slowly turned. There was a hint of sound, for which Fanier had been waiting. Holding the suction clamp, he now withdrew his hand from Steve's face; at the end of the suction disk was a small cylindrical tube. He placed a padded basin beneath the tube as he carried it to an immaculate workstand. He transferred the tube to a plastic plate where another tube of the same size waited. Then he moved an electrified magnifying glass over both tubes. "Steve? Anytime you're ready," he called to the man who now had a hole in place of a left eye.

Steve stood beside Fanier as the technician worked with miniaturized tools. His fingertips, huge and stubby and ridged with pores, broke down the tube into a tiny camera.

"The equipment you've had in your eye, Steve, has been considerably improved," Fanier explained. "You had the capability of visible light or infrared film with a speed up to two-hundredths of a second. Anything over four feet was automatic infinity-focusing."

Steve nodded, waiting for Fanier to continue.

"What we've done is increase the cartridge capacity. You

49

used to have twenty exposures, now you have thirty-two. The film size is the same." He nudged a cartridge no larger than a fly. "Everything else has been modified. Not so much a new design as an across-the-board improvement."

"All I need is my union card."

"The film now takes its exposures at about two-hundred-fiftieth of a second. Same light-sensitive cells attend to the exposure. If you remember, Steve, the old film was Six-X. We've gone up another 50 percent on the ASA rating. . . . One more thing. We've sort of pulled off a little miracle with the film. I said there were thirty-two exposures. There are thirty-two exposures, but each one is split into normal light and IR light, so we'll get sixty-four pictures back. All clear, Steve?"

"Clear. Screw it back in." He turned and went back to the chair, waiting. He knew the rest of it. To activate the camera he pressed against the side of his head, where a trip switch was imbedded beneath the plastiskin that had been built around his once-shattered eye socket. This released the shutter mechanism. To take a picture he merely blinked his eye. This had taken some extra doing for a while. The muscles had been severely bruised, there had been atrophy of the natural internal system and . . . he pushed it from his mind.

When Art Fanier finished inserting the new camera into his left "eye," Steve found himself impatient to finish the job. He had never really become accustomed to opening parts of his body for the strange and at times lethal devices which were as much a part of him as his bionics systems. Bionics . . . cybernetics . . . cyborg . . . words to *them*. To him a way of life.

CHAPTER V

"THIS WILL be our last meeting. Your equipment is ready for boarding. We're sending you to Lima by commercial jet. You'll fly from Denver to Los Angeles and pick up a straight-through flight to Lima. We've arranged a charter flight from there to Ayabaca—the airplane will be a Convair turboprop and should take about ninety minutes."

Goldman studied the group in front of him. The five who would make the expedition to track down the mystery of the energy behind the enigmatic highway discovered by the now-deceased Major Dutch Ryland ... not to mention the forces behind his death.

Steve Austin. Dr. Rudy Wells. Dr. Harold Jennings, archeologist. Phil Wayne, electronics specialist, optics craftsman, photographer. Aaron Mueller, State Department representative.

51

"You've all met," Goldman continued. "You'll get to know one another during this meeting and on your flight to Peru. Once you're in Ayabaca you ad lib, but understand now that Steve Austin heads this expedition. *Mr.* Austin is boss-man."

Goldman looked over his audience. The State Department man, Mueller, was clearly annoyed at the deception implied in the civilian designation, but said nothing. "The matter of Major Ryland. Until his death we had figured this mission for nothing more than a grueling movement in the field. The area surrounding and involving the Cordillera Vilcabamba is one of the most dangerous and treacherous in the world. It's bad enough and challenging enough. But now we have this new element. You know Major Ryland was flown by air ambulance to Norton Air Force Base in California. We wanted him there for its excellent medical care and to give us a secure place to find out from him what happened after he bailed out and found his mysterious highway.

"Before you ask the question, no, neither OSO nor the Air Force maintained any special security for Ryland. There wasn't any good reason for it. Aircraft have flown over the area before. The C-130 in which Ryland was an electronics and surveillance systems officer has been used for years in many parts of the world, often in response to other governments' requests to map isolated areas or areas with special weather or terrain problems. Whatever was photographed or radar-recorded was to be given to the government of Peru.

"Obviously, what Ryland found in the high country is what brought on his death. On the face of it, it's difficult to figure. You know reports of mysterious roads in South America aren't new. But consider again briefly what Ryland saw. A road more than thirteen thousand feet up where there's never been any evidence of human inhabitants. Then there's the composition, the nature of the road ... well, any surface as ancient as this must be, that has a marblelike consistency, has to be of interest. And Ryland did mention, in his interrogation

52

in the hospital, that the road surface likely was not marble but rock fused through some enormous energy. And the shape of the rock . . . the great pieces of stone were not precut to fit and matched together. Not in this road—*if* it is a road. The rest Ryland reported is in your papers."

Goldman paused for a drink of water, cleared his throat. "Now, you know how Ryland made it back. Keep in mind that when he was held at Ayabaca for a rescue aircraft he was feverish. He rattled around in that fever and they couldn't keep him quiet. What he had to say could be expected to pique someone's interest. But enough to cause his death? It doesn't seem to add up. And when you consider that someone might have come all the way from Peru to California and—"

"Or," Rudy Wells broke in, "ordered the job done by phone."

"Right, but in any case the question is what in those hills could induce someone to go to all that trouble, to commit murder? We immediately ran a thorough check. Our counterpart in Peru is Colonel Simon Viejo of Peruvian Army Intelligence. He sent people into Ayabaca. The only item that could be considered out of the norm was some trading activity under way with some companies from Europe. Their visits to Ayabaca are sporadic, and it could be coincidence they were there. Could be.

"We do know the search for an unusual energy beam, of what nature we *don't* know, has been under way in South America for many years. How huge rocks were ever brought to heights of ten to seventeen thousand feet by a people, or by different groups of people, who didn't use the wheel, is still a matter of conjecture.

"The question asks itself. Did Ryland discover something that suggested such energy beams? We don't know. Perhaps the fever interfered with his memory. Partial amnesia resulting from tropically induced fever is not that rare."

"You said this Peruvian intelligence officer—"

53

"Colonel Simon Viejo, Mr. Mueller."

"Thank you," Mueller said affably, in some contrast to his earlier attitude of annoyance. "You said Viejo sent people into Ayabaca. Did they report anything about those European trading outfits that would be of interest to us?"

"I said it could be nothing more than coincidence, but at the time Major Ryland returned from the jungle there were on hand in Ayabaca two men who aren't normally there." Goldman flipped open a folder. "One was Odd Fossengen, a Norwegian national. He owns his own international trading company and he also represents a consortium of major importers and exporters . . . some of the companies represented are from such countries as Czechoslovakia, Rumania, Poland and Finland. Is there a connection between Fossengen and Ryland? If there is, we can't find it. Is there any significance to his representation of a power bloc that would be most interested to obtain any such energy device if such exists? If so, would they go so far as to commit murder in the manner and place they did? If there is hope for discovering such an energy device, would Fossengen, if he's involved, proceed on his own, hoping to sell to the highest bidder? I mentioned two men. The other is Julio Ruperez, a Peruvian national who has worked for about four years with Fossengen. We've checked out both Fossengen and Ruperez, for *any* sign of involvement." Goldman shook his head. "None was apparent. Both men, by the way, were in Ayabaca at the time Ryland was murdered."

"Any records of telephone calls from Ayabaca to the States?" Philip Wayne asked.

"We checked it out, of course. It's not possible to make a call from Ayabaca itself. No direct lines exist for patching through the call. One would have to go to Cuzco. Neither Fossengen nor Ruperez did so. It's certainly possible they had someone else travel there, to make such a call, but that's

54

supposition. We're checking, though. But why kill Ryland—the question persists. Of course one can assume that whoever was behind it was aware of the memory problems that could be brought on by fever. They could have assumed that what Ryland told them would be blocked from his conscious mind for some time afterward, but that drugs and treatment *could* bring it back. So get rid of Ryland before that happened. They would then have the advantage of knowing more of what Ryland had to say than we do, and *if* he did have something to say when he was in Ayabaca, it could be more significant than we realize . . .

"Trouble is, what we're doing is stringing together different possibilities with some rather weak ifs. Truth is, we simply *do not know.* I suggest, though, that you bear in mind that if there is an effort on the part of those unknown to us who killed Ryland to discover this alleged energy source, then your presence will most likely draw them out." He paused. "That's essentially why you're more heavily equipped with weapons than would normally be the case. And it's overwhelmingly why Mister Austin will be the leader of this expedition."

He closed his folders and dropped them into his briefcase, snapped it shut. "Gentlemen, we're running out of time. From here out control of this mission goes to Mister Steve Austin."

"The first thing," Steve said, "is to be sure you're able to survive. We're going into rough country—heat, humidity, undergrowth, mountains, isolation . . . the works. First stop—the obstacle course. No applause, please."

It was just past midnight when Steve Austin led four exhausted men into a small business jet chartered by OSO for the flight to Los Angeles. Steve grinned as the men who would soon be hauling their packs into the high Andes dragged themselves to seats, strapped in, waved away the offers of coffee and sandwiches and abandoned themselves to blissful nonmovement. All except the State Department's Aaron Mueller were soon fast asleep.

Mueller had proved a pleasant surprise. Beneath his abrasive coloration he proved to be tough, determined and in excellent shape; Mueller had kept quiet about his experience as a mountain climber—for a surprise, and the honor of the Department, he said to an impressed Steve. He had even outpaced Phil Wayne. The scene had been nearly hilarious with Rudy Wells, a startling figure as he stood at the beginning of the obstacle course in his own version of Peruvian expeditionary splendor: gleaming green trousers tucked neatly into jump boots, a striped shirt open at the neck and adorned with a bright-red paratrooper's scarf. On his back was a well-distributed seventy pounds. At his hip the .38 revolver (wisely, he had inserted the machete into his backpack to keep it from skewering him). In his hand was the modified deer rifle, and atop his head, directly over pilot's sunglasses, an Australian-style bush hat complete with fanned-out feather. Steve stared.

"Shut up and let's go," Wells told him. "The honor of the profession is at stake."

Steve only hoped he didn't overdo it.

Phil Wayne was anxious to test and prove himself against the others. He was quite a package—an electronics specialist and self-described "rock-hound" who got interested in the subject when he began working with crystals as applied to electronics. "Besides," he had told Steve, "I've done plenty of time in the mountains of Colorado and around New Mexico so I don't think you could lose me if you tried." He'd do. In any case, Steve would pace the expedition by its weakest physical link, Dr. Harold Jennings. Tennis and golf didn't quite add up to the conditioning a man needed for where they were going.

He would restrict Dr. Jennings to a pack of only thirty pounds.

56

"Just so long as you don't prevent me from making this expedition. There is much about this that has drawn me for a long time." His eyes became intense. "People are familiar with the Aztecs, the Mayans, the Inca. But the Caya? Well, they have been too little attended to. They have been, really, not much more than a rumor. It appears there is more reality than rumor. I am delighted—and determined to learn more."

Mueller, in surprisingly good shape, got an eighty-pound pack assignment. So did Phil Wayne. Rudy Wells was affronted when his pack was pared down to sixty pounds, and Steve didn't improve his friend's disposition when he explained within earshot of the others that Wells was really carrying a load of ninety pounds, if one added in the mass of pink flesh hiding beneath his belt.

Jim DiMartino had packed Steve's gear to a weight of one hundred and fifty pounds. Phil Wayne shook his head in disbelief. Mueller just stared, and Dr. Jennings wondered if someone had made a mistake in computing the weight. Rudy Wells busied himself elsewhere to avoid questions only he or Steve could—but wouldn't—answer.

Seated now in the plane bound for L.A., Steve was reasonably satisfied with his group—and had no time to worry about it if he wasn't. He idly watched the blue taxi lights of the airport sliding by his window as the Sabreliner turned onto the active. In his mind Steve went through the procedures with the two pilots, reciting to himself the final elements of the checklist, the verbal exchange between cockpit and tower, the final turn onto the active. He felt the fingers of his right hand clench, then flex as they grasped the imaginary throttles. The jet swept smoothly down the runway and as the pilot rotated the nose wheel off the concrete, Steve felt his body stiffen. Unaware of the movement, he nodded to himself as the gear thunked into its wells and the doors slapped closed. They banked, the airport lights snapped into view, and he had a glimpse of the glowing beam from the rotating beacon. Only then, as they rushed into the night, did his fingers loosen.

"You just don't know when to quit, do you?"

Startled, Steve turned his head around. In the dim glow of night lights, he saw the smile on Rudy's face.

"I thought you were asleep."

"Me? Sleep in a plane? You know I hate to fly."

CHAPTER VI

"I DON'T remember a single thing about that flight last night. I don't remember taking off or coming down or landing. Absolutely nothing until you woke me up in Los Angeles." Dr. Jennings had just seated himself next to Steve, coffee and pipe in hand, shortly after takeoff from Los Angeles for the flight to Lima.

"We aim to please, doctor. Take advantage while you can."

He smiled, then turned to stare at the ocean six miles below. "What do you know of the Caya?" he asked Steve without looking up.

"That's the so-called lost race we're looking for, isn't it?"

"Yes," he said, and turned to face Steve. "As distinct from the Inca, the Mayan, the Aztec—in fact, from all other groups or tribes or races or societies. Distinct at times in only subtle ways, because certainly there had to be some intercourse in ideas. The priests, if no one else. Or their medicine people, who needed knowledge beyond their own capacities. But the Caya were unto themselves, to be sure."

"How did you come on the Caya?"

"I never have. No one has. It's really all a matter of supposition, inference, extrapolation. There have been too many wondrous things not accounted for in the *known* societies and races, *somebody* else influenced the civilizations we have managed to find and study. There's a thread between many of these departed societies and races that can't be ignored—feats of construction, especially at altitudes where such work would have been impossible through manual effort, and certainly they did not have machines."

"Depends on how you define a machine," Steve said. "What do you suppose, doctor, will be the reaction of visitors from some other world if they land on the moon, near the site of Apollo Fourteen?—that's the mission Al Shepard and Ed Mitchell flew. Know what those other-galaxy astronauts will find? A two-wheeled, ungainly, hand-pulled cart, a sort of lunar rickshaw. It will be the only thing at the Fourteen site with wheels. Now, here's a remnant of a society with the power to transport three men and their machines from one world to another, but too dumb to figure out how to build a powered vehicle with wheels."

"I never thought of it that way. You've given me a fresh perspective, Steve. And what about the landing sites of those first two missions—Eleven and Twelve? *No* surface transportation of any kind. But what you said about Fourteen is something to think on. We who will be ancient history to *our* visitors used the wheel for a hand-powered vehicle, but not as a machine. The similarities are fascinating."

Jennings leaned forward, excited. "We know that the past civilizations of South America who built empires and then vanished apparently had incredible—by our lights—powers to move stone blocks weighing twenty, forty, more than a hundred tons—blocks that were shaped and measured with extraordinary care. *How* they moved and shaped and built their edifices is still a mystery today. But one thing we do know . . . *none of them used the wheel for transportation."*

"Because they didn't know about the wheel?"

"No. The toys, the things they made for their children, even the small jeweled sculpture they made for their homes and temples, *did* have wheels. Don't you see the parallel, Steve? If someone examined the landing site of Apollo Fourteen, they'd face the same problem!"

"They certainly would," Steve said.

"What's really important for me, Steve, is that you may have given me a new way to look for things where we're going. I realize that perhaps the Caya can't be proved to have existed. Not yet. But a first sign of what *may* have been the Caya could be this strange roadway reported by the major who was killed. It opens possibilities . . .

"You know, I've been fascinated by the whole structure of what took place thousands of years ago, perhaps even longer than that, in South America. For such a complex and carefully structured society to vanish is hard to accept. What I'm looking for, I believe, is beyond artifacts and constructions. I'm looking for the challenge, the key to intelligence these people *must* have left behind. They *must* have . . ."

"Develop that for me some, if you don't mind."

"What we've seen on the sites of these ancient people represents the homes and the public buildings of what surely were great civilizations. Let's use the singular or collective for the sake of this admitted theorizing. . . . Good morning, Dr. Wells," Jennings said as Rudy Wells joined them and motioned for him to continue.

"Well, I was about to ask, rhetorically, what is the greatest mystery of this ancient people. What they left behind, what we poke through today, tells us nothing about the people themselves. It's frustrating. And can it be accident alone that nothing of the humans who peopled a vast continent has been left for us to try to understand them?"

Steve smiled to himself. Jennings was on a podium somewhere, but he was giving them an insight they'd not be able to get as fast elsewhere, and he was grateful for it.

"Throughout Europe, Africa, the Orient," Jennings went on, "we have found what we needed to reconstruct pretty well how people lived, even how they thought. But from the sun kingdom? Silence.

"Whoever these people—the Caya, or whatever we choose to call them—were, they built structures that rivaled or surpassed other ancient races. But only those of the sun kingdom buried themselves in some vault beyond our understanding.

"They were able to create highways, or roadways, of material similar to macadam—but not macadam—that rivals the best you'll find in highways today. It's there. I've walked it. These roadways were never built less than twenty-four feet in width, often as wide as thirty-two feet. They run straight and true with consistent elevations from one city complex to another. They built their highways across chasms, rivers, gorges, and even swamps. Now how did they build *suspension* bridges carrying the loads we find in modern structures? They built stone embankments that even today baffle engineers. They knew about the wheel but, as I've said, chose not to use it for transportation.

"They built a city on top of a mountain—a city built of stone quarried thousands of feet *below* the city. *How* did they build their city, without the wheel as tranportation and using stone blocks weighing at least fifteen tons, cut so smooth that even today a knife blade can't be slipped between those unmortared joints?

62

"And there is proof these people charted the planets. They mapped the intricate rotation of the solar system and they did it with greater accuracy than any other people before Kepler's time. I have studied their stone carving of a man seated in front of a long, tubular object mounted on a tripod, and looking into the sky. The telescope. Where did they get the lenses?"

"I thought," Steve said, "they didn't have optics."

"That appears to be the case," Jennings replied. "No optics. No sign, ever, of optics. No signs of grinding. No suggestion even of glass. A blank. And yet here is that bas-relief of a man seated in front of a telescope."

Rudy Wells broke in. "And their reaction to Cortez and the Spanish is remarkable. The records are rather clear on this. They seemed to know that Cortez represented disaster for them. And they accepted his arrival as the working out of whatever providence they believed in. They knew he and his men would destroy them. Not Cortez personally, but the forces he represented. Their religion apparently offended the priests who accompanied Cortez. Their conversion efforts were not gentle persuasion. The conquerers were out to do more than banish the local idols. They went after the compiled records, everything in writing. They burned out all the years these people had achieved. Later generations had only the legacy of the mumbling of the withered shamans of their own people and the newcomers' so-called culture. Except by then, of course, the Spanish weren't newcomers. They ruled everything with an iron hand. Only what was in stone, and only a part of that, could survive."

"There's something else, Steve," Jennings said. "It's been my theory—and I've not got too much company here—that these departed people estimated accurately the intelligence level of the Spaniards, and then left a record for some future generation to read that was beyond the capabilities of their conquerors. It's been wrapped in silence for ages—an enigma in a riddle of time, so to speak. Anyway I just don't believe they destroyed everything. Again this is theory on my part, but I believe the intelligentsia of these people took their own lives. There was no way—they seemed to have an ability or thought they had an ability to foretell the future—that they could resist the alien social structure represented by the Spanish. They couldn't survive against their gunpowder, their military discipline. In any case, if they did intentionally remove themselves from the scene, it would seem that, like the Japanese they prepared well for their exit and removed nearly everything that could tell us about them. Nearly, not completely. Somewhere on the continent the key waits for whoever can decipher the instructions."

Wells moved into the conversation again. "There's some who believe the Caya behaved like the Egyptians and built a huge pyramid or temple that conceals a vault or chamber with their secrets—in this case, secrets kept from the Spanish. Maybe we ought to look for a rosetta stone."

"I hope one of you is an expert on ancient languages?" Steve said.

"I don't believe it will be language," Jennings answered quickly. "I suspect it will be with a device, or a tool, or some kind of equipment that only a well-advanced society—such as ours would appear to the Caya—could interpret."

"Can you take that any further?" Steve asked.

Jennings nodded. "Well, I think the clue is in stone. The Caya revered stone. They revered what they could do with stone, its strength and durability. They did not have metal alloys as we know metal. In a very advanced way theirs was a stone-oriented society. So a people who left behind them—visibly, anyway—only stone would reasonably be expected to use that stone to conceal their holiest treasures. Remember, theirs was a sun kingdom. They used stone to reach to their greatest heights. I believe the two must link. If there is this hallowed place of theirs, then I think it will be in stone."

"And when and if we find it," Rudy Wells said, "look out. Presumably they also knew how to protect what they wanted hidden."

Jennings nodded agreement. "You know," he said, "that these ancient people were truly a warrior people. They weren't afraid of death, they were used to it. They were proud, fierce. And yet they never fought Cortez. Why did they permit themselves to be slaughtered?

"The records do show that the Incas showed resistance to save their leader from degradation. And that resistance? First they apologized to the Spanish for not obeying them, and then soldiers in rank after rank stepped forward for voluntary slaughter. Offering their bodies and souls in the place of their leader. They didn't try to save the life of the man who led them. What they seemed to want for him was the right to select his own means of death rather than have it forced on him by the Spanish. An act of superiority, you might say. Perhaps even arrogance.

"In any case," Jennings finished, "hardly indicating a people to be underestimated."

CHAPTER VII

THEY STOOD in a small crowd, staring. "Well, there she is," Steve said, finally, grinning at the others.

"You mean we're going into the high country in *that?*" The disbelief and shock in Aaron Mueller's reaction was matched by Phil Wayne's and Rudy Wells's.

"How about you, Dr. Jennings?" Steve asked their archeologist. "No complaints?"

Jennings smiled. "I'd ride a mule to get where we're going."

They sat on their packs and luggage. The object of their restrained affection, waiting for them when they'd landed at the main airport of Lima, Peru, at a height of thirteen thousand feet above sea level, was the airplane assigned to their expedition. It was parked at the far end of the field, away from the commercial terminal. Not exactly hidden, but far enough into the boondocks of the airport perimeter to attract at most a passing glance. An ancient Douglas C-47, descendant of the DC-3 twin-engine airliner that went into commercial service in 1935. The venerable Gooney Bird, beloved veteran of war, crosser of oceans and reliable iron bird of mountain passages. In its time and for years after, probably the greatest airplane ever built.

"Okay, a few words so we keep our story straight," Steve said. "This aircraft is officially registered to the University of New Mexico, which is also the official source of all our funds for this fishing trip. You're all on the record as having received a grant for this journey. We have an open account with the federal bank of Peru. Mueller will run that part of our operation, so if you need anything take your problems to him."

Mueller got up from his improvised seat, walked beneath the high nose of the C-47. He shook his head and turned to Steve. "Look, you've no doubt seen the logs on this machine. Mind telling me how old it is?"

"Date of manufacture is 1942."

"My God," Wayne broke in, "it's older than I am."

"How many hours?" Mueller pressed.

"Twenty-eight."

"Twenty-eight hundred hours?" Wells said. "That isn't too bad."

"Twenty-eight *thousand,*" Steve corrected.

Rudy was incredulous. He turned again to survey the ancient flying machine. The paint had peeled in various places across the wings and fuselage and tail. Oil streaked the bottom of the engine cowlings and the wing undersurface. Wells didn't want to see anymore.

Phil Wayne said, "Look, Austin, I've done some flying myself."

"How many hours?" Steve was studying Wayne with more than casual interest.

"Oh, about fourteen, fifteen hundred. I'm just a private

jock, really, but I did work at it. Still do, for that matter. Sometimes when you know a little it's enough to scare you. I know this is a great old bird, but we're at thirteen thousand feet. This thing is going to need ten miles to get off the ground if she's carrying any kind of a load. How are you going to operate from short grass strips at this altitude or even higher when this . . . this thing can hardly get out of its own way on *this* field, which is paved and has good winds down the runway?"

"Leave your gear where it is," Steve told all of them. "Come aboard. I've got a few things to tell you." They trooped into the airplane, leaned forward to climb the angled floor toward the cockpit, crowded about him until Steve motioned Wayne to the copilot seat on the right side of the flight deck.

"All right," Steve told him, "you people are going to fly with me in this bucket. Not just fly. We're going into the tall country. We're going in where no sane man would fly a machine like this. The Gooney Bird, great as she was and is, was never designed for operation at the altitudes in which we'll be working, just like Phil said. But I'm glad to tell you that this rusty old bucket is a sham. Gooney is not what she seems to be." He pointed through the side window at one of the two engines. "The Gooney Bird that everyone knows has two engines, each delivering twelve hundred horses. Not *this* Gooney." He patted the throttles. "Beneath those cowlings out there we have under each hood no less than eighteen hundred horses. Thirty-six hundred total—almost twice as powerful as the standard bird. More to the point, those new engines fit within the old cowlings. No additional drag. Phil,"—he turned to Wayne—"take another look at those props."

Wayne peered through his side of the cockpit. "Well . . . hey, I see it now. They're much fatter. You know, thicker than the standard blades."

"Right," Steve told him. "There's more than power under

those cowlings. There's some rather special supercharging. We get sea-level power all the way up to seventeen thousand feet. *This* Gooney has better performance at seventeen grand than a standard Charlie Forty-seven at sea level. Also all new control surfaces. Couple of things you don't see with the naked eye. Better balancing, greater area, faster response. The flaps look the same but they're not. They give more than twice the lift of the older airplane. Also, something we'll use when we really need it. Leading-edge flaps. Just like the big iron birds without props that make all that noise and smoke. You're all familiar with the 707 and the Boeing line. Remember how the leading edge of the wing comes alive for takeoff? Well, this old baby here has all those things going for her. And for especially tight spots, the bottom of the fuselage, just forward of that belly antenna, there's a pack with six rocket bottles. They'll really push this thing off the ground."

Steve got up from the seat. "Phil, stay right where you are," he told Wayne. "In that side pocket against the bulkhead you'll find the pilot's handbook on this thing. Start reading. You've just been made copilot—"

"Steve!"

He turned instantly at the sharpness in Rudy's voice. The doctor was by a left cabin window, pointing to the ground. Steve turned to his own window, looked out. By their gear, studying everything carefully, moving the packs, was a man they'd never seen before.

"Mueller, please move your diplomacy out there quick," Steve told the man from the State Department. "Keep him occupied. Talk to him. You're the specialist at foreign relations."

Mueller looked at him briefly, turned and was gone. Through the windows they watched Mueller walk up to the stranger, who looked up, startled, then broke out a wide smile and extended a hand.

70

"He recovers fast, anyway," Wells observed.

"Too fast," Steve said.

Jennings looked at him. "You sound as if you know the man."

"Never met him, but I'll predict he knows us, who we are, at least something about what we're doing here. And I'll bet I know who he is too. It's just that he surfaced a lot sooner than I expected."

Rudy Wells turned from the window. "You wouldn't be talking about a certain Norwegian, would you?"

"You mean the man Goldman told us about?" Jennings said. "That fellow . . . Odd Fossengen. Is that it?"

"The same," Steve told him. "By now Mueller should have shaken him out of his cover. Let's go meet the man."

Both men turned as Steve and the others emerged from the plane and approached them. Mueller was civil enough, but Steve could tell he'd been frustrated by an operator smarter than was expected.

"Steve, this is Mr. Odd Fossengen," Mueller began.

"Mr. Fossengen," Steve said, taking the outstretched hand. He made no move to introduce anyone else.

"A pleasure, sir," Fossengen said. Steve took a moment to size up what he saw. Fossengen was a big one, one of those heavy-set men with noticeable jowls surrounded by a thick neck and powerful shoulders. He wore dark glasses—a wise move at this altitude, where the sun burned more brightly than at sea level—but behind the glasses Steve could still see the eyes moving to take things in quickly. A very alert individual. Steve noticed something else—his hair, very blond, very frayed at the ends.

"Why don't you tell us what you were doing?" Steve said.

"I don't understand," Fossengen said.

"Sure you do. You were digging through our gear."

71

"My apologies," he said. "I did not mean to give the wrong impression. I spend so much time in the back country. You have the latest equipment, I was interested. Anyone who goes into the back country would be. You understand? We help one another out here."

"How'd you know we were going into back country?" Steve said, deciding to ask a dumb question and let this man feel superior—maybe then he'd loosen up a bit and inadvertently reveal something.

Fossengen laughed as he pointed to the assembled pack gear. "Where else, Mr. Austin, where else with all that? Anyone would know where you were going. In fact, I would say you intended to fly that machine to Ayabaca."

"You know a lot about someone who's just landed," Steve said.

"No, by no means a lot," Fossengen said. "I have been hoping for someone like you, Mr. Austin." He turned to point across the field. "Over there, see? The red-and-white machine, the Aztec? It is mine but it has a problem—a new valve is needed for the left engine. It will take several days. Here in Lima"—he shrugged—"one does not expect swift delivery of parts. So I cannot fly my machine, and there is none at this moment available for rent or charter. So I go to the air-control center. All flights out of Lima are controlled. All those that go into the back country are even more strictly controlled. And I ask my friend in the center, does he know of anyone who will be flying that way? Someone with whom, perhaps, I may find room for myself and a friend. I am, as you say, hitchhiking. And my friend in the traffic center tells me the crew of a Douglas has requested weather information for the area east of here. Ayabaca lies that way, true?"

"Yes."

"Well then"—Fossengen extended his hands—"You see? There is nothing mysterious about it after all, and I am most urgently in need of such transportation. I would also be very glad to pay the way for myself and my friend, Mr. Austin."

"I can't help you," Steve told him.

Silence, then: "I do not understand." An edge to his voice now.

"I'd like to help but"—Steve jerked a thumb at the C-47—"that aircraft belongs to the University of New Mexico. They've got rules. Our insurance, for example, doesn't cover anyone who doesn't work for the university."

"But we will sign any waivers, the risk will be all mine, all ours."

Steve seemed to be wavering. "Fossengen, I'd really like to, I really would, but I can't do it. If the university people ever found out I'd be looking for a new job the next morning. Sorry," he finished, shaking his head, then grinned quickly. "But my good friend here, Dr. Wells, he'd like to buy you a drink, I'm sure." He glanced at Wells. "Rudy, why don't you walk Mr. Fossengen back to the terminal and buy the man a drink on us?"

Rudy picked it up quickly enough, moved forward and linked his arm with Fossengen's. "Is it true what they say about gold in the Andes?" he was heard saying to Fossengen as Steve and the others watched them walk away.

Aaron Mueller turned back to Steve. "Congratulations," he said, "and I mean it. You handled that very well. By the way, the man's a fake."

"I know," Steve said, "and so is his name. He's not even a Norwegian."

Mueller—Jennings and Wayne—showed their astonishment. "How do you know *that?*"

"Well, once a long time ago I dated a girl—a brunette—who lived in Denver. She was a brunette, but she had this thing about being a blonde. Real fixation. So she dyed her hair as blonde as that man who just walked away from here. And she

73

had the same problem as he does right now. I said she lived in Denver, more than five thousand feet above sea level. Thin air. Cold. And too much dye used too many times to keep her a blonde. The ends of her hair, Mueller, split so badly that after a while she lost most of her hair. Did you get a good look at Fossengen? He's no more a Nordic blond than you are."

"Then what is he?" Jennings asked.

"Bad news, for sure," Steve told him. "Look, you people start stowing our gear aboard. We've got a truckload of equipment to get into this bird. I didn't want Fossengen or whatever his name is watching what we load. Rudy should keep him occupied long enough for us to do our job. I'm going over to the freight office to have a truck bring our stuff here."

The three men by the airplane watched him leave. "You know something?" Mueller said, "I'm beginning to be sold on that man."

CHAPTER VIII

~~~~~~

THE VILCABAMBA hung on the distant horizon like a saw-toothed wall built by giants. From the small cockpit of the old C-47, Steve in the left seat and Phil Wayne in the right, Rudy Wells standing in the doorway immediately behind and between them, the mountains seemed slowly to drift toward them, lifting gently but steadily as they did so. The altimeter needle was pegged at twenty-two thousand feet, and for the moment they enjoyed calm air. This was the time in flight when movement of the airplane to human senses seemed to be suspended completely. The airplane was a capsule sealed off from the rest of the world. There was no sensation of movement. The panorama of a mighty mountain range assumed a new dimension, and the men felt as if they were a tiny pod floating through a sea while the distant world came to them. Even the sounds were muted, the engine roar a distant murmuring. Human bodies had become attuned to the vibrations of the machine and, in harmony, no longer resisted such forces and paid little or no attention to them. Ordinary flight became a magic carpet. Was the wind just outside that glass and that thin metal skin really shrieking past at some two hundred miles an hour? And the temperature . . . the outside gauge had crawled steadily around the dial to register forty degrees below zero on the Fahrenheit scale. Yet within this thin-skinned cocoon it was warm, comfortable. There was only one acquiesence to their environment. Each man had a lightweight oxygen mask strapped to the lower part of his face, and their voices had the metallic ring of radio intercom. For some time now no one had spoken. In the cabin, Dr. Jennings slept soundly, well strapped in. Aaron Mueller sat with his chin cupped in one hand, staring through a side window. The three men clustered within the nose of the old airplane yielded to the sights before them. Mountains of splendor were changing shape before their eyes, were emerging from haze and slanted sunlight to become individuals in their own right. And then they were over the Vilcabamba, approaching across its central flanks. At the same time they saw the sweep of clouds from their side, a thick layer of tumbling cumulous racing in to obscure the peaks.

"Better look while you can," Steve said. "Apparently we came in here during one of those rare breaks. In a couple of minutes . . ."

In the brief moments of clear sight they looked down, awed by the tumbled and jagged rock faces and peaks below them. The mountains were dark; rock that was black and dark brown, tinged with traces of deep red, and in the distance, with shades of gray-blue. Nothing seemed to live down there, not tree nor shrub nor bush. Just rock, naked and forbidding, with the only life clustered along its lower flanks, looking from up

76

here, at their height, like moss clinging desperately to its host.

Well ahead of them, and to the south, its flanks already covered by the fast-moving wave of clouds, they could make out the blunt peak of El Misti, a thin spray of steam or smoke, or a mixture of both, issuing from the crater. The wind whipped immediately at the plume, flattened it at once, tore it away. Steve eased the C-47 into a gentle turn to the right. He wanted to come in to Ayabaca well to the south, heading due north, so they might have a good look at the lower heights—lower by comparison only with El Misti—where they hoped to begin their search.

Steve turned to Rudy Wells. "Go back and wake up Jennings. I want him to have a look at the area. First impressions can be important, and we may not have this kind of break in the weather for a while. Tell him to come up here."

Rudy disappeared. Almost at the same moment they hit the first shock in the air, the wind blowing and tumbling away from the peaks. Steve glanced at Wayne, but he was already snugging his seat belt and shoulder harness. Wayne glanced at him and nodded. Good man, he thinks ahead.

Jennings poked his head into the cockpit. "Doctor, there's a jump seat right behind me," Steve told him. "Get in and strap yourself down tight. It's going to get a bit rough up here." Jennings followed instructions, hauled his lap belt secure and grasped the seat ring behind Steve for added security. In just those few seconds, as the old transport moved deeper into the mountain air wave, they were taking sharp blows of turbulence. For a few moments Steve debated with himself about Phil Wayne flying through the area. He'd had time in light twins but nothing near the size of the C-47. Given ten or twenty more hours he could break in Wayne, but now wasn't the time.

"Phil, get that special chart out for Dr. Jennings." Steve moved the control yoke from side to side, gently, the pilot's signal that he had the controls. Wayne held up his hands and pulled the chart from his case, spread it out for Jennings to see.

Steve held the Gooney Bird in a long turn until they were due south of towering El Misti. They were still in a break with the weather, although it surely wouldn't last much longer. The transport shook from nose to tail as the C-47 was displaying her unhappy tendency in rough air to wallow from side to side. Steve wondered just how long Rudy would last before he admitted the inevitable and hastily swallowed some motion-sickness pills. Or made a dive for a plastic bag. Either way the good doctor was sure to be unhappy. Then they were in perfect position.

They looked forward with the terrain unfolding before them as it did on the chart. "Dr. Jennings, you've got the volcano clearly?" Jennings studied the chart for a moment, nodded, pointing at the high peak far ahead of them.

"Fine," Steve said. "Now, directly before El Misti—you'll have to look sharp because of those lights and shadows through the clouds—can you make out two other features? The one closest to the volcano is Temple Mountain. You can barely see it."

"I—I think so," Jennings said. "Binoculars would help, Steve. I've got some in my pack and—"

"No, doctor, the way this thing is bouncing around, all you'd see would be a blur. Well, look, check the position on the chart. You can hardly miss the Chalhuanca Plateau. It's directly between us and Temple."

Jennings stared ahead, referring back to the chart, then nodded. "Got it. It's . . . like a butte in our southwest but much larger."

"About ten times larger than anything we've got."

The clouds had split the afternoon sunlight into huge beams poking down from the mists, magnificent pillars that seemed to glow from within. One huge shaft of light reflected brilliantly off water far to their left.

78

"Got that?" Steve pointed to the reflection. "Okay, check it out on the chart, doctor. That's Puma Lake. A lot like our own Crater Lake in the northwest. Exploded and blew away most of the mountain."

Steadily the gross details spread along the surface of the earth enlarged before their eyes as they closed the distance to their objective. There was another way to look at the area that held their interest. Closest to them, nestled within a bend of the Sicuani River, was the town of Ayabaca and, directly across the river from the town, the grass airstrip. The river ran in a general east-west direction to the east of Ayabaca, in lush jungle foliage. Small mountains, many of them better described as large rolling hills upthrusting from the verdant country, were everywhere. But as you progressed northward from the river, the ground sloped rapidly. Perhaps it was once a major range with the abrupt rise one found from Death Valley in California, straight up the rugged slopes of the Sierra Nevada. A sharp peak, a sort of miniature Matterhorn, lay directly before them, east of Ayabaca and north of the river. Beyond this peak, unnamed on the chart but which Steve decided to call Matterhorn because of its obvious name-reference value for his group, rose a larger, blunt-shaped peak. Although it was too far to make out any details at this distance, Steve knew—and pointed out on the chart to Jennings—where the small town of Azul was located. Where Major Ryland had stumbled down from the hills, feverish, swollen from insect bites, in agony from a broken arm.

He pointed out Cerro Pumasillo with its peak 9,124 feet above ground. "But"—Jennings protested—"that plateau, the Chalhuanca . . . it appears to be thousands of feet higher than Pumasillo. That's, well, hard to believe."

"Start believing, doctor," Steve told him. For several moments he withheld conversation as the transport crashed into an invisible turbulence. The left wing dipped sharply and for a long, sickening interval they hung nearly vertical, the

79

airplane rattling through the sudden fall. Steve let the Gooney have her head; no use fighting that kind of whooping downdraft. He felt the controls begin to grab again. "Hang on," he called to the others, and brought in full right aileron, ready with the rudder, bringing back to almost its full stop the yoke in his left hand. The Gooney shuddered and banged metal together and then they were out of it. Only occasional beams of light now pierced the clouds, and the air was making it impossible for a novice to do more than hang on for dear life.

"Guess that's it," Steve told the others. "Dr. Jennings, it's too rough for you to try to get back to your seat. I think you'd better stay up here with us."

Jennings gasped. "Will our—what did you call it?—old bucket survive all . . . this?"

"All this and a lot more, doctor," Steve told him. "Remember, they used to use these old coal haulers for crossing the Hump in World War Two."

"Hump?"

"The Himalayas. And it was a lot rougher than this." Steve glanced at Wayne. "Phil, crank in the radio to one twenty two point eight."

"Unicom?"

"That's what they've got at Ayabaca. Tell them we're twenty south and coming down from nineteen thousand."

"Right." Wayne busied himself with the radio contact. He pressed the headset close against his ears and had to repeat their call sign several times. Finally he turned to Steve. "We're cleared in. Surface wind at fifteen knots gusting to thirty-five. Down the runway at two zero zero."

"Sounds like it's on the nose."

"Yeah, no local traffic, they say."

Steve came back on the power and the C-47 eased into a steep descent at two thousand feet a minute. The others would be blowing like whales to clear their ears, but they'd had enough time at it lately. The transport shuddered and slewed as Steve brought them down through the punch of the winds streaming from the distant peaks. Then they were through the worst of it. Steve had Ayabaca clearly in sight. Grass surface, four thousand feet long, no tower—just someone looking out the window of the operations shack.

"Check me on the elevation," he said to Wayne.

"Thirty-two hundred."

Five thousand feet on the altimeter. "Half flaps," he called to Wayne. His copilot brought the flap handle down, dropped them to 50 percent. They slowed their speed, feeling the deceleration. Steve called it off. Gear down, full flaps. He was on flat pitch on the props, playing the throttles, bringing her around in a steep curving descent so he could roll out on their final approach.

"Going to use those leading edge flaps?" Wayne asked.

"We don't need them here. We'll turn off before we ever reach the halfway mark."

"That," Wayne said after a pause, "should be something to see."

Back some more on the power, the bumps lessening. The runway dropped neatly into sight dead ahead of the nose, and Steve came back even more on the power. He brought her low over the trees, dragging her in, and behind him he could hear Jennings sucking in his breath. He sensed Wayne tight as a steel drum by his side, fists clenched in his lap, determined to sit it out without a sound. When she began to shudder with the first indication of the coming stall, Steve brought in power. The big engines rumbled smoothly, helped by those fat blades on their props. The airspeed indicator trembled around seventy, and their sink rate eased off with a slight nudge of more power. The last trees whispered beneath them. They were all holding their breath, teeth clamped tight, sweating

81

out what was to them the inevitable crash. The runway rushed toward them and at just the right moment, the only moment, Steve moved the yoke forward *just* so much, and tapped in power. The Gooney Bird lowered her nose, grabbed at the angel's whisper of lift, and touched the wheels without a sigh.

"I don't believe—*look out!*" Wayne's shout was still in his ear as Steve saw the truck rush from a clump of trees on the side of the runway directly before them. His hands moved in a blur. Full power, the throttles jammed forward ahead with back-slamming acceleration. Not enough. Without conscious thought, every move one of reaction rather than planned action, Steve hit the lever for the leading-edge flaps.

Lift. Lift from flaps and power and the speed they had left, even the lift from ground effect—the air-cushioning between the wings and the ground—and it was all together just enough to carry the C-47 forward and up in a crazy bounce and they were over the truck and beyond. Steve chopped the throttles, slammed her down on the grass, standing on the brakes as he swerved to the right. Phil Wayne flinched as the trees rushed to his side of the airplane but he had no more time to think of it because Steve was standing on the left brake, the left only. He brought in full power again to the right engine, the prop screaming as it spun with maximum revolutions, and in that wild, deliberate movement, almost an out-of-control ground loop, the C-47 swung around to the left, reversing its movement and rushing back along the airstrip toward the truck.

"Mueller!" Steve called out. "Your rifle! Get it and get ready to bail out of this thing."

He brought in power to the left engine and raced toward the truck now stopped near the right side of the runway. A man gaped from the truck cab. They watched the vehicle jerk forward, stop. "He's flooded it," Steve said. The man stared at the huge prop rushing at him, then bolted from the truck and

82

rushed for jungle cover off the runway. Steve brought the transport around to the right. He stopped with the cabin door in full view of the truck and the running man.

"Mueller! Get out there and get him!" Mueller, out of his seat, moving fast, threw the door handle and flung open the stops. He dropped from the airplane to the ground, the rifle in his hand.

"Stop!" he yelled, his rifle cracked, a sharp report echoing along the runway. Mueller had fired over the man's head. Steve tore away his straps. "Hold her with the brakes," he yelled to Wayne, and ran down the cabin, wheeling through the door to Mueller's side. There was a glimpse of a form just disappearing into concealing brush.

Angrily he jerked the rifle from Mueller's hand, brought it swiftly to his shoulder and aimed. The rifle came down slowly. Too late. He turned to Mueller. "You had him nailed. Why didn't you do the job?"

Mueller looked at him. "Austin, that would have been killing a man, an unarmed man, in cold blood."

"And just what do you think *he* was trying to do to us . . . he nearly did us all in and you—" He tossed the rifle back to Mueller.

"Austin, did you ever stop to think," Mueller said, "that what happened could have been an accident?"

Steve looked at him, turned and went back to the airplane.

CHAPTER IX

"I'M GOING into Ayabaca—the town's across that river," Steve told them, "to check in with the local authorities. That's part of our deal. I also want to talk with whatever passes for the local constabulary to file an official report on what happened out here when we landed. Dr. Jennings will want to have a few words with a local office that deals with guides for this area. And then we're coming back, before nightfall. When we get back, you people will have your rifles loaded with a shell in the chamber. You'll have put together a hot meal for all of us—use the galley in the airplane . . . Someone tried to take us out today. They missed, which doesn't mean they'll quit trying. This airplane is an easy target on this field by itself. So are we. Tonight we all stand watch."

85

They returned shortly before nightfall. It was either cut their visit to Ayabaca short or stay there the night through, and Steve wasn't about to leave that airplane with three men who might hesitate and get themselves killed before they could pull a trigger. "That ferry is on a cable," he explained. "They use a pair of mules walking around a windlass to haul it back and forth. The old man who runs it won't stay after dark. He says maybe falling into the river at night isn't worth it. Chances are you don't come up alive. We'll find out more in the morning.

"Tomorrow Jennings and Wells have to be in Ayabaca. Mueller, you'll go along to ride shotgun, and even if you're touchy about using that rifle you should be able to discourage any unfriendly types in broad daylight. But be back here by three in the afternoon. No later ... Rudy, you and Dr. Jennings will want to talk with that local guide office. They know the country better than anyone else, and—"

Rudy broke in. "You never said anything about using a guide."

"And we're not going to. We can't trust anyone here. We have no idea who's been bought by Fossengen. Also, a guide has a mouth. He'll either sell his information to the highest bidder or maybe talk just to make himself a hero. But I want you to talk with them. Nose around. Anything you pick up could help. Call it window-shopping. Mueller, you register with whoever passes for the local chief or government man in Ayabaca. We'll play this straight up, just like you said from the start." He turned to Wayne. "Phil, you please read up on that handbook. The more I think about it the more I'm convinced we may need someone else to fly this tin beauty. Didn't you say you had about fifteen hundred hours?"

Wayne nodded.

"How much multi?"

"About four hundred. You know, Cessna 310, Aztec. But

I've got about two hundred hours in the Twin-Bonanza."
Wayne grinned. "And three hours in the right seat of the
airplane I'm sitting in right now."

The Twin-Bonanza, Steve reflected. Husky airplane for its
size. Same basic procedures as the Gooney Bird. Stepping
from one to the other was a matter of thinking a little bigger.
With that much time behind him, plus the fact that Steve had
judged Wayne as more than competent, he could check him
out to handle the C-47 through the complete takeoff and
landing routine. He'd pick it up with Wayne in the morning.
"Phil, go over to the airport office. We've got maybe thirty
minutes of daylight left. Let's get this thing tanked up before
dark. Have him bring the gas truck here, and make sure he
drains the sumps on that truck before he runs a hose to our
tanks. And then watch him. Wear your thirty-eight like it's
high-noon time. In full view. Check the fuel yourself. And the
oil."

Wayne got to his feet, opened his pack, strapped on the
revolver, withdrew the weapon and loaded six shells into the
chamber. Steve nodded with satisfaction.

He turned to the others. "Chow time. Everything ready?"

"Sorry I left my chef's cap at home," Rudy said. "Field
rations coming up."

"Good. Keep Wayne's hot for him. Mueller, soon as you
eat, sack in. Get your rest now. You're on guard shift like
everybody else."

"I didn't ask to get out of it," Mueller said.

"Good man. Never volunteer."

Steve went into the cockpit by himself, closed the door
behind him. He knew his move would raise some uncomfortable questions. No way out of it; besides, he could probably
offset curiosity with an edge to his voice, pretend irritation.
Cut off from the vision of the others, he took out what ap-

peared to be a set of heavy flight goggles from his flight case. Careful examination showed them to be something more— micro-miniaturized electrical circuits were embedded in the goggles. He closed a twistlock wire lead to the frame, ran the wire within his clothing down to his right leg. He pressed a detent he felt with his fingers, and a section of the bionics limb slid away. He worked in darkness, by feel. The other end of the wire was another twistlock, and he inserted this within the power capsule in the leg, twisted it into position. The panel came back into place. He brought the goggles up over his face, sat erect in his seat and looked through the cockpit windshield.

A ghostly world of infrared lay before him. He saw by temperature emission from whatever came within his sight to a distance of about a thousand yards. Without the IR goggles the airfield lay shrouded in gloom. He draped the goggles carelessly about his neck and returned to the cabin. Wayne, Jennings and Mueller were there. Phil Wayne waited expectantly for him, Jennings puttered with his equipment, Mueller was asleep in the cargo area, his body pushed against parachute packs. Steve motioned for Wayne to help him remove the wide belly hatch, one of several special modifications for the Gooney Bird. They lifted the hatch, placed it quietly to one side.

"Got your pack?" Wayne nodded, and Steve motioned for the other man to follow him. They dropped quietly to the grass beneath the transport. "The truck first," Steve said. "Try not to make any noise."

Wayne's hand held him. "Where the hell is it? I can't see a damn thing out here."

Steve brought the goggles up to his eyes. "Put your left hand here," he instructed, moving Wayne's hand to his right shoulder. "Stay close with me." With no further word Steve started across the field. The grass was cool and dark to his infrared vision, but the truck, still radiating heat from its metal, came to him clearly against the "cold" background of foliage. When they were almost there, Steve slowed, tapped Wayne's arm. "Can you see it now? About twenty feet away."

"How the hell do you see in the dark?" Wayne asked in a whisper. "Those goggles?"

"You're the electronics genius. You tell me." He hoped that would take care of it.

Wayne nodded. "That I will. When we get back."

"Can you work without light?"

"Sure." Wayne worked his way forward until he touched the truck. "Okay from here. You play watchdog." He disappeared beneath the truck. Five minutes later they were on their way back to the airplane.

"Okay, let's get the rest of it set up," Steve said. "I'll give you a hand." They busied themselves in a wide circle extending to a hundred feet on all sides of the transport, placing small tripods on the grass at sites selected by Wayne. Finished, the electronics specialist set up a panel in the cabin. "Done," he said, wrapping it up. "The pattern on this board roughly matches the perimeter. Wait, I've got an idea." He fished in his equipment kit and with a piece of chalk roughed an outline of the C-47 on the plastic-faced board he'd just completed work on.

"Great," Steve said. "Now sack in. I'll get you up at three A.M. for your shift." Steve outlined the setup to the other three and draped his body in a cabin seat. Seconds later he was fast asleep.

"Steve, wake up." Steve broke out of sleep, sat up abruptly. "It's on the alert board," Rudy added.

Steve glanced at the panel. Where Wayne had outlined the airplane and the circle beyond he saw three glowing red lights. "Get the rest of them up and stay low," he said as Rudy moved away. Moments later they were by his side, looking at the panel. "You all understand it? Each red light marks where someone has broken the photocell beams Phil set up around us. About a hundred feet away from the ship. They must be working their way in slowly. I suspect they'll start after us with the truck they left here on the field. Okay, everybody to positions."

Cargo parachutes had been placed by several windows. In each C-47 window was a twist-out plastic shield; once removed it yielded a space through which a rifle could be placed—holdover from past wars when troops were given a psychological boost to shoot at attacking enemy fighters. No one ever shot down a fighter with a rifle, but shooting was better than chewing nails. The cargo chutes were the equivalent of sandbags, providing cover for the men at window positions within the airplane.

"Rudy, take that window. Dr. Jennings, you get to the right side. Remember, you already know their general position. No shooting until you hear one of us open fire first. Mueller, you come with us."

Steve knew those waiting outside would concentrate on the hatchway that the door had been closed against. Let them keep watching. Each man had the long clips in his rifle and had thumbed his weapon to full auto. Steve slipped down through the open-belly cargo hatch and went prone on the ground. Wayne and Mueller followed, spreading out quickly, staying prone. They knew what to do.

They didn't have long to wait. In the darkness across the field, they heard the truck motor grind to life, then roar suddenly as the driver raced the engine. No lights yet. They heard the truck coming around to face the airplane, picking up speed, and abruptly the bright headlights stabbed on, exploding night into dazzling light. Steve didn't watch the truck. Neither did Wayne or Mueller. They were looking in the direction where the photocell alarm had shown them people were waiting. The plan wasn't that hard to figure. At full speed the truck would smash into the tail of the airplane, doing enough damage to ground the C-47 several weeks. The men inside, shaken by the unexpected blow and movement of the airplane, would come rushing out through the cabin door. . . .

Steve glanced at the luminous dials of his watch. Forty seconds. The truck engine keened as the driver kept the accelerator floored. Forty-three seconds; Steve looked out into darkness. The headlights rushed toward them. Forty-five seconds and the plastic explosives charge went off beneath the fuel tank of the truck. Flame went skyward, followed by a smashing explosion as the tank blew. Garish light was in all directions. Men totally surprised by the blast reacted. They moved, lifted their heads, sprang up from prone position into a crouch.

The men by the C-47 opened up. One rifle from the cabin, fired by Rudy Wells—short, clipped bursts. Steve took aim on a momentarily illuminated figure, squeezed off a short burst. Arms were flung out and the form crumpled to the ground. Wayne and Mueller fired steadily. Another figure tumbled.

"Hold your fire," Steve called. Guns went silent. The ghostly flames of the burning truck sent long shadows across the field. In the distance, staying low, barely visible, a small group of men were running off, and for a moment Steve considered going after them. He decided it wasn't worth the risk. They'd done enough damage to make the survivors think hard about trying again while they were on the field. And the ones who got away would at least slow down a little the ones who wanted the airplane destroyed and its occupants shot down.

Steve thought about that a while. One name—Odd Fossengen. Too many things tied together, going all the way back to Fossengen's presence when the natives carried Major Dutch

Ryland down the river from Azul to Ayabaca. That, and his presence at Lima when they landed, and his cock-and-bull about needing transportation. Plus that he was anything but Norwegian.

Steve began to think more seriously about what might be waiting for them in the mountains. Whatever it was, people were willing to kill anyone who got too curious about it.

They couldn't have gone very far the next day even had they planned on starting their mission. Not with a charred corpse in the seared wreckage of the truck. And especially not with four bodies found the next morning on the airfield. In their favor was the attempt to wreck the C-47 on their first landing and their immediate report of the matter to the local police in Ayabaca. The police who came to the airfield found the four men gunned down by Steve and his crew exactly where they had fallen. With their rifles. And with dynamite.

Steve left the matter to Aaron Mueller. Word came back from the Peruvian government that Austin and the others were in the country by invitation, that their papers were in order. It took two days for the Peruvians to be satisfied that whatever actions had taken place were in self-defense and for the Americans to be cleared of all charges.

Left hanging were the reasons behind so strong an attack, involving as many men as had participated in the move to destroy the C-47 and, if necessary, its occupants. Several times the word "gold" came into the conversation, and the Peruvians went along. It was more than plausible. There had been many expeditions in the past that had pretended archeological interest and instead had concentrated on rumored hordes of gold and precious jewels. A made-to-order smokescreen for the real purpose of Steve's expedition.

The delay for the investigation also gave Steve two full days to run Phil Wayne through a grueling, accelerated checkout in the airplane. By noon of the second day Phil was handling the C-47 with confidence.

The third day after their arrival at Ayabaca they moved out. Into the highlands. Fossengen no doubt eventually behind. Ahead—who really knew?

CHAPTER X

~~~~~~

STEVE CAME across the Chalhuanca Plateau an even thousand feet over the high tableland beneath them. It was an eerie feeling; it didn't seem right to be flying at 17,000 feet with all that flatland directly below, only a thousand feet away. There wasn't any question of their altitude. They were all wearing oxygen masks. The Gooney Bird took a lot of power and a big box of airspace to make its turns. Holding his altitude of a thousand feet, Steve dragged the Chalhuanca from the four points of the compass, checking everything in sight. He didn't like the winds. They seemed never to blow at less than twenty miles an hour. He was beginning to believe this was a constant diet for the plateau. It could make life miserable for them. Even on the ground, when they would have to work, they'd be sucking oxygen periodically to keep their heads from spinning. It would take some time to acclimate their systems to the thin air.

He came around a wide turn and said, "Dr. Jennings, it looks as if the plateau was once a lot bigger than what we see now."

Jennings was standing directly behind him. "I agree. See there, along the western edge? It's almost a vertical drop to the lower valley. It looks like a granite upthrusting, but . . ." He shook his head. "It doesn't feel right."

"And there hasn't been enough time for erosive wear like we find in Utah or Nevada," Steve added. "I'd guess there's been some heavy volcanic activity here and most likely strong earthquakes."

"As well as very erosive rainfall." Jennings leaned forward for a better look as Steve swept around the vertical walls of the western slope of the plateau. "Except for the eastern ridge," he went on, "it seems to be close to vertical all around. And to the east there's been some severe erosive damage. Steve, just how are we ever going to get up there? From what I understand, if we worked our way as far upriver as we could, it would still take us another ten days to two weeks to reach the plateau. And then we'd have to start climbing. That could take another week—or more."

"We don't walk, doctor. And we sure don't climb, because we haven't got three weeks." He pointed to what showed as a level expanse of green along the side of the plateau. "See that open area down there? It looks pretty good. If it turns out to be as good as I think it is, we're going to land there."

A moment of silent disbelief. Finally a sound over the intercom, from Rudy Wells back in the cabin. "Did I hear you right? You intend to land this thing *down there?* Steve, the altitude's got you. Check your mask to see if it's working. You—"

"Don't worry about it, Rudy."

96

"What the hell do you mean don't worry? You don't know what's down there. For God's sake, Steve, we're so high we'll come in too hot and . . . oh, what's the use."

Phil Wayne was nodding. "I think he's got a point, Steve," the copilot said. "I mean, you really can't tell what's in there."

Steve came around in a steep turn, coming back on power and starting downstairs in a slide of diminishing altitude. "Let's go back to the field," he said. "I'll lay it out for you."

At first light next morning, before the winds began their steady rush across the Chalhuanca, the C-47 rose again from Ayabaca field, climbing steadily for altitude. This time Phil Wayne sat in left seat as the aircraft commander, with Steve in the copilot seat. Wayne had been told to climb to 18,000 feet and to circle the plateau. At ten thousand Steve left the cockpit, waving Jennings into the right seat. He went back into the cabin, where a dour-faced Wells and a tight-lipped Mueller waited for him. "Steve, listen to me," Mueller said. "You're taking an awful chance. Not just for Rudy, but yourself. There's got to be another way to—"

"Let's not waste time," Steve said, "and thanks just the same, Mueller, but this is the only way. Doc, hook up to a walk-around bottle." Both men disconnected from the cabin oxygen system and plugged into an oxygen cylinder attached to their belts. "Mueller, it's a bit cramped in here. We'll need your help."

His protest made and obviously not going to have any effect, Mueller did what was needed. Steve and Wells slipped into parachute harness, a single backpack. Each man was assisted by Mueller, then Steve and Wells checked each other out in every detail of their gear. They put on jump helmets and gloves, hooked a static line from their chute pack to the overhead cable running the length of the cabin. "We're going out the belly hatch, Mueller. Secure yourself with that safety harness, and then pull the hatch for us."

The hatch came back and dust flew for a moment through the cabin. "Phil, you read me?"

"Got you, Steve."

"Make a pass from east to west. Just off the centerline of that field down there. I want to drop a marker."

Rudy sat against the side of the cabin, trussed up in his gear, feet splayed out stiffly, watching everything, not saying a word. Steve braced himself by the open hatch, looking down. "Coming up on the run," Wayne called.

"Right. Hold her steady as she goes, Phil." The pin came out easily from the smoke bomb and Steve dropped it through the hatch. Halfway down to the open grass field smoke burst from the bomb, forming a long streamer that continued to impact. Then smoke poured forth in a thicker cloud, bending before the wind. "Good," Steve said quietly, "right down the field. Phil, around once more, and when you come in again for the same pass, use half flaps and ease her off until you're indicating ninety."

Wayne's voice was terse. "Roger. Nine zero indicated."

"Good. I'll call it out at five seconds for the first jumper." He turned to Rudy, motioning him to get ready. Wells stood by the hatch, facing forward. They rolled gently through the turns, leveled. They could feel the speed easing off, the slight rumble when half flaps were brought in.

"Right down the line," came Wayne's voice. "Ninety-five coming down, we're on ninety."

"Hold her right there," Steve said. He was a bit worried about Rudy, but he dismissed it with the knowledge that the doctor had gone through the rigorous, even brutal, paramedic training and had jumped into worse than this. The question of altitude had been his greatest worry. If they jumped with a regular chute, even the biggest 34-foot canopy available, they wouldn't have directional control worth a damn and they might drift right off the edge of the plateau. And if they landed on target, their descent speed, especially in that wind, could even more easily snap a leg bone.

They weren't jumping regular chutes. Each man wore a Paracommander, a chute intended for special control in spot landings and able to handle altitude nearly as well as a regular chute would operate at sea level. The Paracommander flew as part-wing, part-chute, and coming down into the wind they could reduce their speed over the ground to nearly zero. That's what the book said, anyway. The highest elevation Steve had ever jumped—ground elevation—was eight thousand feet, and this was twice as high. Well, no time like the present. He made sure Rudy was in position, moved in right behind him.

"Five seconds," Steve called. His hand smacked Rudy's thigh. Rudy dropped through the hatch. On hitting the airstream he spread-eagled his arms, legs apart, in the classic sky-diver's position to balance his body. Almost at once he whipped away from sight. Steve was out the door a second later. The icy wind slammed into him, started to tumble his body. He was moving into the sky-diver's balance when the static line snapped taut. The chute ripped open, a tremendous jerk grabbed his body and whipped it around. Then the silence of falling beneath the open canopy. Somewhere in the distance he heard the fading sound of the C-47 engines.

He reached up to grasp the two wooden steering toggles with which to maneuver himself. There were only seconds left. He caught a sight of Rudy's red-and-white chute as the doctor swung downwind, coming around in a curving descent, as Steve himself was doing, so that they might come down into the wind. The wind dropped its speed to what felt like fifteen miles an hour. Rudy several seconds before him, Steve worked the toggles to bring him directly into the wind and touched down at near zero speed over the ground. He took the landing upright, staying on his feet, watching Rudy playing it safe, feet together, his body folding expertly along the ground. Both men moved swiftly now, running forward to collapse their chutes. They worked their way out of their harness. Rudy ran toward him. The air was mean cold, the wind biting, and Steve was grateful for the oxygen bottles they breathed from. He reached into his pack and removed a walkie-talkie, pulling off his jump helmet as he did so.

"Poppa to Little Bear, we're both down safe," he called to Wayne in the circling transport.

"Hey, great. We saw you hit." He laughed with relief. "Okay, Little Bear, let's get with the rest of it. I'll give you two smoke bombs on a direct line for your drop."

"Got it, but don't miss," Steve cautioned. "Those things can't steer." He looked up as the wind freshened, flattening the tops of the waist-high grass about them. "Phil, make your drop at five hundred above us. You copy?"

"A bit low, isn't—"

"Five zero zero," Steve said.

"Got it."

"Okay. Smoke going out." Rudy was already pulling two smoke bombs from his pack. He handed one to Steve, who ran down the grass field about seven hundred feet from Rudy. He waved to the doctor and both men pulled the pins and dropped the grenades. The smoke poured forth in a perfect marker for the transport. On the first pass a heavy pack dropped away neatly, the chute opening almost at once. Fortunately the wind held true and the chute came down a hundred feet within the first marker. The second drop was off, close to the edge of the plateau, but the chute snagged in a small gnarled tree and they had the equipment.

Steve and Wells went to work at once. Steve drove a steel rod deep into the ground. Not as deep as he wanted; it struck rock about eight inches down and stopped. He judged it would hold, and unfurled a bright international-orange banner at the top of the rod for a marker. Carrying three more rods, he and Rudy walked the length of the grass field. No rocks underfoot. Beneath the high grass, surprisingly solid footing, a surface leveled by centuries of strong winds and erosion control by the grass. Much of the plateau was deceptive. On the way down in the chute Steve had caught a glimpse of sun reflection along the western edge of the tableland; that indicated water of some kind, and also very possibly a mosslike surface that could be spongy and treacherous.

It took them an hour. By then they'd marked off 2,800 feet of fairly level ground covered by the high grass. They'd changed oxygen tanks near the end of that hour. The C-47 circled now at twenty thousand. Steve called Wayne. "Phil, by the best we can measure, we've got about twenty-eight hundred feet of good material for you to land."

"Doesn't seem like much, Steve. Not at this height. We'll be coming in pretty hot."

"If I didn't think you could hack it you wouldn't be up there. Now kindly shut up and listen. The wind's doing about thirty and it's right down the centerline of the area we marked out. You set up your approach well out. Bring it in with gear and flaps down—you know the routine—and flat-pitch those props. You can be generous with the power. Hold her on ninety-five indicated."

"You guys look like you're standing by a tennis court," Wayne complained.

"It's bigger than it looks. Now, if you feel you can't make it the first time in, *go around.* Keep your nose level and pour the coal to her. But I don't think you'll have to do that. We'll give you smoke for a wind-marker."

"Steve, the boundary for touching down . . . could you cut away some of that grass and give me something to shoot for? Otherwise it looks like I'm coming down on water. That grass has no depth perception to it."

"Not a bad idea." Steve pulled a machete from the equipment bag, saw Rudy doing the same. "Hey, doc, you sit this one out." He'd gauged correctly just how tired Rudy was—the jump alone was enough to wear out a man at this altitude. Rudy sank gratefully to the ground with his back against their equipment pack. Steve closed the hand of his bionics arm about the machete handle, and for ten minutes the steel blade was a blur as he slashed away a strip through the grass a hundred feet wide and thirty feet deep.

"Okay, Phil," he radioed. "No more horsing around. Bring her in now. By the way, if you're worried about overrun, the surface beyond the outer marks is spongy moss. You won't get very far. C'mon, kid, time to graduate."

Wayne swung the C-47 well downwind, banked steeply as it turned through base and onto the final. Wayne was calling out the steps as he went through the procedures: gear, flaps, leading-edge flaps, power, altitude, speed, rate of descent. Steve was in the cockpit with him, knowing and feeling every move, talking to Wayne.

"You're in the groove," Steve called as the Gooney Bird presented an almost dead-on view to him. Then he saw it drifting off to one side. "Phil, crab her in. Don't make any gross corrections. Crank in some left rudder and she'll be true blue long before you get here."

Wayne came in just a hair below the speed Steve had called for, but he was really dragging grass and this compensated. "Chop power," Steve shouted into the radio as the transport loomed before him, rushing toward the ground. "Keep that yoke back and work those brakes!" In the cockpit, a white-faced Wayne followed the calls, the throttles snapping back, the yoke hauled as far back as it would go to get the tailwheel down, combining ground drag with the angled wings as she rolled three-point. "Watch the brakes," Steve cautioned. "The moment you feel that tail coming up, ease off and then put 'em on again."

The transport stopped less than fifty feet beyond the outer flags. A lovely job.

They spent the next few hours taking it slow. They taxied the airplane as far back to the eastern part of the improvised strip as they could park it safely. Rudy ordered everyone to eat—hot soups, which refused to get really hot because water boiled at such a low temperature at their altitude, and high-protein rations. And he insisted on candy bars for all hands after that. He ordered a regimen from then on of eating and drinking.

Finally, with Steve taking guard watch, they slept like the dead.

Steve woke the others just before three o'clock that afternoon. Wayne and Mueller set up the photocell detectors several hundred yards from their camp area, which consisted of the airplane and strong tents pitched beneath its wings. Steve found some disbelieving glances about this order, but was too tired to argue. "Just do it," he said, irritably, and out of his sight Rudy motioned to the others to stop arguing and get on with the job. For a while Steve assisted Rudy and Jennings in setting up the camp, hammering tent stakes deep into the ground. The afternoon was gone by the time they finished, and Mueller and Jennings forced themselves to eat before they crawled into their tent and in effect passed out. There was much to do, but any excessive effort at this altitude, Rudy warned, and they'd be incapacitated by nosebleeds and headaches, to say nothing of wheezing lungs.

They passed the night quietly, taking two-hour guard watches. In the morning, immediately after breakfast, Dr. Jennings brought everyone running to his side with a sudden shout. He stood by a surveying instrument, waving his arms.

"We're onto something! I—I—" He was turning a pale blue before their eyes, his body suddenly wavering from side to

103

side. Cursing, Rudy ran to him, unbuckling an oxygen mask, slapping it to Jennings's nose and mouth, helping him to the ground. "Five minutes, doctor," Rudy warned. "Don't talk, don't move. Whatever it is, it'll wait five minutes."

Jennings tried weakly to gesture, and Rudy lost his temper. "Lie still, dammit, or I'll put you out with a needle." Jennings groaned, but closed his eyes and lay silent. His color returned as his breathing improved. The moment Rudy released him, with a warning to take it slowly, Jennings stood up and pointed to the west.

"There," he said, the excitement now controlled. "Puma Lake. See it?"

"I see it, doc," Wayne said. "It's as big as a mountain. How could we miss it?"

Jennings ignored the needle. "Do you notice the line of our impromptu airstrip? We're centered here on the plateau, and our strip runs *exactly* east and west. I want to stress that. All the peoples of South America that built complex structures in a relationship *always* functioned on the cardinal points of the compass. It was always due north or west or south or east. I've never seen nor heard of any deviation from that."

Rudy Wells nodded. "That's the way I found it in Bolivia, too. The roads there, I mean. Dead along a magnetic compass heading."

"Of course," Jennings went on, his excitement drawing a warning from Wells, "and that road, the road or highway, or whatever it was that Major Ryland found, *must* be on this plateau. We're not along its centerline, but much of this tableland has eroded away. Much has been lost through earth tremors that must have broken away the flanks. To the south looks doubtful. But directly to the north of us ... see, both Temple Mountain and El Misti are on an *exact* magnetic heading of due north. I don't believe the volcano will fit into any of this, because it could be comparatively recent—it shows

104

signs of young birth, and there's every likelihood it came into existence long after the roadway was built."

He stopped talking to breathe in deeply, as Rudy again offered the oxygen mask. Jennings went on. "We might, if erosion and other damage hasn't wiped out all traces, find some indication of a road that also leads to the north. We just may be standing near the crossroads of what was an ancient and totally unknown empire. The home of the Caya!"

They found the road minutes before the sun slipped beneath the mountain peaks far west of the Chilhuanca Plateau. Jennings was right. It lay along what was the northern rim of the tableland. They had time only to verify its existence, and for Rudy to order Jennings, white-faced from excitement and overexertion, back to their camp.

"But I can't leave it *now,*" Jennings said. "I've been looking for . . . for this"—he was assailed by a fit of coughing—"all my life."

"Doctor," Steve said quietly, taking him by the arm, "this road has been here at least ten thousand years. It will be here in the morning. What you don't know is what lives up here or visits this plateau at night. We've found game trails all over the place. That means a feeding ground for big cats. Maybe jaguars. The night is their time. It isn't yours. Now please come back to the camp."

Jennings stared at him, suddenly feeling exhausted beyond the point of quick recovery. "Of course, you're right."

Steve nodded. "Tomorrow, Doctor Jennings."

They returned to camp, where Rudy placed an oxygen mask to Jennings's face. The scientist was asleep before his head reached the pack he used for a pillow.

It rained all night. The kind of rain that is described in mystery tales. A wind howling at more than forty miles an

105

hour, the rain slashing at them almost horizontally. And still Steve insisted on the guard watch, with the exception of Jennings.

In the morning they discovered they'd had company during the night. And no one had seen a thing.

CHAPTER XI

~~~~~~~~~~~~~~~~~~~~~~~~~~~~~~~~~~~~~~~

"WHAT HAPPENED?" Steve demanded of Phil Wayne. They stood by the photocell tripod that made up the eastern corner of their electronic alarm system on the Chalhuanca Plateau. A dozen feet from the tripod they'd discovered the broken grass that aroused Steve's suspicions. He followed the faint signs and stopped when the footprints became visible beyond question . . . visible despite the heavy rains, because whoever had come up there during the night had penetrated the rain-soft soil. The water drained off, leaving—just long enough to be detected—the fading footprints.

"Steve, I don't know what to say." Phil Wayne was devastated by the failure of his device. "I even set up the system with both the optical *and* audio alarm so we wouldn't miss . . ." He shook his head. "It could have been the rain, it was coming

107

down heavy enough during the night, what with that wind and everything ... it could have blocked the optical sensors. Maybe even lightning. There's a chance it could have overloaded the system. I just don't know, Steve. I'll have to check it out close."

"Time enough for that later," Steve said, taking Wayne off the hook. "Luck was still with us." They walked to the rim of the plateau, looked down along the steep slope. "See how the fall is set up?" Steve pointed. "Soft rock, with plenty of outcroppings. And there's heavy bush and vines all through. It looks tough, but a good mountain man could work his way up here."

"In that rain?"

"Depends how good you are. A man coming up this slope, using a light that we'd never be able to see from where we were—" He shrugged. "Point is, someone was up here during the night. I said our luck held out. First, our visitor apparently saw the tripod. He had to figure we'd been alerted. Especially after what happened down at Ayabaca. That kind of lesson sinks in."

Wayne nodded. They walked back slowly to the airplane, where Aaron Mueller was taking his shift on squaring away the campsite. They stopped long enough with Mueller to have warm coffee and tell him what they'd discovered. Mueller sighed, leaning back across the big tire of the C-47. He draped his arms across his knees. "I'm beginning to get the idea someone would like us to go away."

"You learn slow, but you learn," Wayne told him.

"So I'm a slow learner." Steve extended his hand as if for the first time. "Welcome aboard, Mr. Protocol."

No one could ever have faked the smile they got from Mueller. He also got quickly to his feet and took Steve's hand in a firm and genuine exchange.

"By the way," Wayne said, breaking it up, "where's Jennings and Wells?"

108

"Over there." Mueller pointed to a grove of trees a few hundred yards off.

"How long have they been gone?" Steve asked.

"Hour or so. I'll call them on the walkie-talkie."

"No, let's surprise them."

"But we'd be leaving the plane unguarded. Shouldn't one of us stick around?"

"Not in daylight," Steve said. "Whoever's after us works best in the dark." He led them off toward the heavy growth.

They came on Jennings and Rudy Wells on their knees, examining an extraordinary smooth surface beneath them. A powerful battery-run fluorescent light was a pool of glare between them. Jennings was studying the road surface with a thick magnifying glass, while Rudy worked industriously to chip away a section of the material. Strewn about them were the tools of Jennings's trade—and their rifles. For a couple of minutes Steve, Mueller and Wayne watched them. There was no sign that their presence was even suspected—Jennings and Wells were in their own world.

"This is a stick-up," Steve said, his voice flat. Jennings froze where he was, his face still poised over his magnifying glass. For a moment Rudy went rigid, then went for his rifle. As his fingers closed on the weapon Steve placed a foot on the barrel. Rudy looked up, his expression going from chagrin to anger.

"That was a pretty stupid thing to do," he said to Steve. "I could have—"

"You could have had your head blown off and never known it. What's wrong with you? An elephant could have come up without either one of you knowing it."

Jennings's eyes were bright with excitement. "*You* attend to security, Steve. Right now my mind has no room for anything except *this!*" His hand swept wide to take in the surface around them.

Steve turned to Wayne. "Phil, will you sort of keep point?" Wayne nodded, and Steve and Mueller bent closer to the two men on the ground. Steve's impatience with Jennings and Wells left him as he studied the roadway beneath the bright flood of light. Now, more than before, he understood.

At first glance it looked, startlingly, like a terrazo floor. It had the same consistency, at least to the eye, and when Steve ran his hand lightly across the material where it had been rubbed clear by Rudy, he found it as smooth as any floor he had ever touched. The texture baffled him and the color didn't settle any easier. It reflected light in a strange manner so that he couldn't really grasp the coloration. From one angle, without moving his head, the roadway—he stopped himself from labeling it stone—gave off a dull, greenish sheen. It reminded him somehow of jade, although he knew that was hardly possible. He moved his head to change the angle of reflected light and the green shifted its hue into a flickering bronze. And then a strange golden red.

"Doctor, what the hell *is* it?"

Jennings, apparently as baffled as Steve, rose from his knees. "I don't know," he said finally, "and the very idea that this material defies me is . . . well, wonderful. I mean, Steve, I have examined basic materials, stone and clay and glass and ceramics and God knows what else pretty much all over this planet. I've been on top of mountains and inside caves. Pyramids, graves, mausoleums, archeological digs of every kind, and I've *never* seen anything like this."

He took a deep breath, and Rudy glanced at him with concern. "Slow down," he warned. "You're getting into hyperventilation. Do you want to pass out again?"

Steve gave Rudy a hard look with his use of the word "again." Rudy shrugged and motioned for Steve to drop it.

"I know one thing," Jennings went on, more slowly now, "if this material once was stone, it isn't stone now. The entire culture is supposed to be based on stone. Everywhere in Central and South America stone is revered, stone dominates, but this isn't stone. It's not glass, or quartz, or marble, or anything like it. The way it twists and bends light . . ." He shook his head. "Not only that, but wherever the road wasn't split by natural forces, such as lightning or earth tremor, in all the thousands of years this roadway has been here, there's been no interference from growth. Do you know what that means? You've seen airports unattended for only a few years. Grass and weeds and bushes sprout up everywhere. That's only the smallest fraction of the time this road has been here, and from the areas we've examined so far, that's never happened here. The seal of this material has proven impervious to heat, cold, atmospheric gases of all kinds, animal droppings with their chemical reaction . . . I don't know of anything comparable in modern technology and—"

"Enough," Rudy broke in. "Harold, I warned you . . ." He lifted an oxygen flask and mask and handed it to the scientist. "Ten minutes under partial pressure. Start now."

Jennings protested feebly, then sat down carefully, bringing the oxygen system to his face. He took several deep, controlled breaths. At their altitude, if one started breathing quickly, then faster and faster in order to suck more oxygen into the system, one could beat hypoxia—which was oxygen starvation—but one was also nailed by its accomplice, hyperventilation. As a flight surgeon, Rudy had lived with this all his professional life, and he knew how to gauge himself. Rapid talking in thin air meant rapid breathing, and what you did then was to start emptying your respiratory system of carbon dioxide. The body needed about 11 percent of the normal lung capacity. Reduce that carbon dioxide level below the figure of 11 percent and the body started demanding a return to normal. The best automatic defense system the body had was to force the whole system into unconsciousness. Everything calmed down and the carbon dioxide level went up again. Sucking oxygen when you were hyperventilating simply flushed out even more carbon dioxide and brought on even faster the swimming sensation into blackout. Knowing such things, having attended men who had succumbed to these dangers, he well knew how to pace his words and his breathing in reaction to where he was.

Rudy had completed his task of breaking free a clear section of roadway, and this had been accomplished only through diligent use of a cold chisel and hammer, aided by his own skilled and powerful hands. He stood before them, all on their feet except Jennings, who hid his chest pains behind the oxygen mask on his face. Rudy gestured with the stone, and as he did so it caught at an angle the light from the fluorescent lamp and seemed to swirl with green and flecks of gold and a deep wine color.

"I think *I've* seen this material before," he said finally. "Or something very close to it. Even the basic coloration, the predominance of green"—he tapped the smooth surface in his hand—"is the same. That's more than coincidence. Not only that, both materials, the one we have from this road, and the other I—"

Jennings found it impossible to remain silent. "What . . . what is it called?"

Hesitancy on Rudy's part, then: "Trinitite." His eyes went to Steve, who looked at him in disbelief.

"Trinitite," Rudy repeated.

"I don't believe it." They turned to look at Steve. "It's impossible."

"It's not impossible. I'm not saying the source of the heat would necessarily be the same."

Steve went quiet, deciding to hear Rudy out.

"Trinitite? I don't think I've ever heard of it," Aaron Mueller said.

"Is it a crystal?" asked Wayne. "I handle a lot of crystals in my business, you know, for electronics and broadcast systems. I don't think I've heard of trinitite."

112

"It's not crystal. And, Harold"—Rudy turned to Jennings—"please stop staring at me. It's not a natural item. But I believe trinitite and this material"—again he referred to the slab in his hand—"were formed the same way. I also think there's no longer any question about the legend we've been chasing down about a strange kind of crystal in the ancient high country of Peru. A crystal that the best of modern-day science can't even understand, let alone *build*."

Mueller turned in exasperation to Steve. "Will someone tell us what he's talking about? This trinitite stuff . . . where does it come from?"

"New Mexico," Steve said. "That was the first place. I've seen it there. I've also seen it at Jackass Flats. And Frenchman's Flats. It's also been found at Bikini, and Eniwetok, and about a thousand feet or deeper in Colorado, and a few thousand feet down in Alaska," Steve went on. "But the first place was in New Mexico. At a place called Trinity."

"Would that be in 1945?" Mueller asked carefully.

"July 16th. At five-thirty in the morning, to be exact."

"The first atomic bomb," Mueller said.

"Atomic bomb?" The words echoed from Jennings, who got slowly to his feet. He turned suddenly to Rudy. "Surely you're not serious!" he exclaimed. "You can't suggest that the ancients had the secret . . . the use of—"

"No, of course not," Rudy said quickly. "Do you know how trinitite got its name? The first atomic-bomb test was given the code name of Trinity. It was a bomb exploded from a tower set in the New Mexican desert. Some time after the explosion the scientists and technicians who carried out the test visited ground zero—the radiation levels were safe by then for a short visit. They discovered that for a distance of four hundred yards in every direction from zero the sand had been transformed by the awful heat of the atomic fireball into a glasslike substance. Its predominant color was green. When you turned it to catch the light from different angles, it shifted colors."

Again he gestured to the material in his hand. "Just like this does."

"In New Mexico," Steve said, "the raw material was sand. The fusing element, what came from that fireball, was unbelievable heat. What we seem to have here"—he pointed to the roadway—"is some raw material—stone, sand, a mixture . . . I don't know—that also was fused by heat."

"Don't you see?" Rudy said. "*Heat.* Fantastic heat. But not from a bomb. Heat that was *controlled.* Energy that was—"

"*Beamed* energy," Phil Wayne said. "It's got to be a beam . . . something like a laser, I'd guess. But they'd need a power source, wouldn't they?" He looked from one to the other. "I mean, you've *got* to have a power source. Rudy, you said something about a crystal. But that's not enough. Where'd they get the power? How could they—"

Rudy pointed upward. "It's been there all the time, Phil. The sun."

"But that's not enough, doc. There's got to be something that directs—"

His words snapped off as if by a thrown switch. They all heard it at the same time. Unmistakable. From above, from where Rudy was pointing. A *plane.* Steve didn't wait to comment. He took off at a run back toward their C-47 parked unattended at the end of their improvised airstrip.

CHAPTER XII

HE WAS in the open near the C-47 when he caught a clear look at the airplane swinging overhead in a wide circle about the plateau. At first he'd missed it. Sighting the plane against a sky filled with scudding clouds—he was surprised to see the first tendrils of mist racing at their own height and even below the plateau—was bad enough. Trying to get it down with the lack of proper depth perception because of one eye made it worse. He stopped where he was, shading his eye against the strange flickering light of the approaching storm, and saw clearly the markings of the Peruvian Air Force on the wings and fuselage. The pilot rocked the wings from side to side in a time-honored gesture. Steve was running again to the base camp beneath the C-47. Moments later he'd tossed a smoke grenade near the left corner flag marker of the airstrip. Bright-orange smoke

115

billowed forth to show clearly the direction and general strength of the wind down the strip. Steve hadn't hesitated to fling the grenade. When local officials want to land, better make it easy for them. They'll come in anyway.

He watched the ship coming around into the wind, flown by a man who was obviously an old hand at mountain flying. He had a good ship for it—a modified Helio Courier; six-seat job with a big Garret turboprop in the nose. Power to spare, and she handled altitude with her big high-lift wings like a huge bird. The Courier was sliding over the grass as the other four caught up with Steve.

"That's an air force ship," Wayne said.

No one else spoke. The Courier landed neatly, the nose high into the wind, came to a stop in only half the distance of the improvised runway. It turned smartly to taxi back and park near their transport. They waited, silent, as the prop jerked to a halt and the cabin door opened.

First from the airplane was a man in military uniform. "I recognize him," Mueller said quietly. "Colonel Simon Viejo. Peruvian Intelligence. Remember the list Goldman gave us? It had his picture."

A second man, older, was helped from the Courier by Viejo. "That's Yavari," Jennings said quickly. "He's the leading archeologist of Peru, probably the best man in his field anywhere in South America." They started walking toward the plane, then stopped as Colonel Viejo leaned in to assist a third person.

Phil Wayne couldn't believe the sight of the raven-haired beauty who stepped from the cabin, wind streaming her hair. Not even field boots and trousers, and a windbreaker, could hide the femaleness of the woman who stood with Yavari and Viejo watching the Americans. "I don't believe this," Wayne muttered, as much to himself as the others. "Who can *that* be?"

Jennings surprised them. "It must be Carla. Yavari's daughter. And from what I've heard, she's quite as capable as her father." He started forward, saying, over his shoulder, "She should be. He trained her."

They watched as Jennings was greeted warmly by the Peruvians. "Aaron," Steve said, "I think you'd better do the honors. This is all we need . . . an intelligence officer, another scientist, and a white goddess. I think I'll kill Goldman when we get back. *If* we get back."

Within fifteen minutes of the Courier's touching down, the sun had been blotted from sight by heavy, low clouds, and looking down from the plateau they could see clouds racing along a few thousand feet beneath them. The temperature was dropping fast, and what had become a chill was now on the edge of bitter cold. The wind was rising, bringing with it an uncomfortable mist. Steve and Colonel Viejo, with Mueller and Wayne trailing, went quickly to the Courier, turned it into the wind and secured the airplane with stakes and tiedown ropes. They carried several bundles of gear from the Courier to the big transport. Then, leaving the two Peruvians and Jennings and Wells in the airplane, to share their common scientific interests, they retired to the larger tent staked out beneath the C-47 wing.

Viejo got to it fast as Steve, Wayne and Mueller listened. Steve had been prepared from the moment the colonel stepped from his airplane to dislike the man. And understandably, he felt. Viejo was here only because there'd been serious trouble: attempted murder and arson, nighttime attacks against guests of the Peruvian government. Add in the gutted truck on the Ayabaca airstrip, the bodies kept waiting for government inspection and autopsy and the fact that these strangers had no sooner come into the Peruvian heartland than they had killed. Viejo—slim, rawboned, with a knife-edged moustache—made it clear he held none of them responsible. But at the same time, he pointed out, they drew trouble like flies.

"My government," he concluded, "really has no choice. To prevent more questions and even a diplomatic problem we must keep with you Peruvian nationals who will remove all question of the propriety of your expedition."

"That seems to settle that," Steve said. "Let's get on with it. From what we've learned so far, our next job is to work our way across the valley to Temple Mountain."

Viejo nodded. "It will not be easy . . . I have the report, of course, of Major Ryland. What he had to say about the mysterious roadway he came across. If it does indeed exist in this area, then the legends of the Caya may after all have truth in them. Have . . . have you discovered anything?"

Steve glanced at Mueller and Wayne before turning back to Viejo. "The roadway"—he gestured across the field—"is about four hundred yards in that direction. It's also an intersection."

"There is no mistake?"

Steve explained what they had discovered, and the conversation among themselves. "In fact, Dr. Wells and Dr. Jennings brought back a piece of that roadway with them. It's in the airplane with Mr. Yavari and his daughter. You can see it—"

"No, it will wait," Viejo said quickly. "Better for Yavari to enjoy the moment before me. This is a dream coming true for him. You will understand there has never really been enough money to support extensive, costly archeological studies. There is just so much to go around, priorities, that sort of thing. But now that this has happened, and we are here . . . it is like the world opening up for him. I must, though, ask a sensitive question."

"It can't be more sensitive to us than those people who tried to kill us."

"Of course. In fact, the question involves, I am sure, those same people. We have had a report that you are looking for precious stones, also gold, and that you have information that could lead you to such treasure."

"Not a word of that story is true," Steve said.

Aaron Mueller broke in. "Colonel Viejo, I'm sure you were briefed on our background."

"There is no question about accepting your word, Mr. Mueller. How the story was created is the problem. The information was presented as coming, so to speak, from the horse's mouth."

Steve laughed. "I'm pretty sure I know where the story originated. Rudy. He must have done a real artistic selling job on Fossengen." Steve then related in detail their welcome from Odd Fossengen when they were loading the C-47 at Lima. ". . . the lost civilization, the jewels, and the gold . . . Fossengen apparently bought Rudy's package."

"I am not so sure," Viejo said. "This man Fossengen has been a problem for a long time. He is dangerous. If I had my way I would either have thrown him out of the country or into jail."

"Why haven't you?" Mueller asked. "After all, when you consider the attack on the airplane . . ."

"But can you prove that? You lack proof for us to move against this man. We have had Fossengen under surveillance for some time. I do not believe he is the efficient merchant he pretends to be. He spends too much money. I can find no way for this man to have stayed in business as long as he has."

"Someone's bankrolling him?" Steve asked.

"I should think so, but he is a very generous man with his largesse—so generous that he has made powerful friends in important places. And since I lack proof—"

"It might help if you told us your thoughts about him," Steve said.

"If he is not the merchant he represents himself to be,

Colonel Austin, then he is a . . ." He searched for the word and Steve proposed, "Front?"

Viejo nodded. "His government—his real name is not Fossengen and he is not Norwegian, although all his papers are in order—is remarkably interested in this area . . . the Sicuani River valley. It hardly has seemed worth all that effort. However, you have just told me you found a section of this roadway, or whatever it is, that until this moment has been only a dream, a theory. What are *you* looking for here, colonel, that justifies all the expense of *your* government?"

Steve had already decided to level with the Peruvian officer. Viejo was cooperating with them. He could have been heavy-handed, officious. So he laid it all out for Viejo: their discussion of the roadway . . . the strange properties of the surface material, its incredible durability . . . conviction that the material could have been formed only by the precision control of enormous energy . . .

Viejo asked questions, often turning to Phil Wayne; it was obvious the Peruvian officer was no stranger to electronic or related systems.

"Well, then, it all fits, doesn't it?" Viejo said when Wayne finished. "Obviously Fossengen, or whatever his true name may be, is interested in more than precious jewels or gold. I do not think," he said to Steve, "that, as you said, he bought your story. It seems he only pretended to do this. The crystal, or whatever we may find, is clearly of great importance."

"Importance," Wayne said, "is understating it, colonel. If the Caya managed to produce a crystal that had that much energy derived from a natural power source—appropriately enough, the sun?—think what could be done with something like this crystal *and* modern electronics . . ."

"I imagine," Viejo said, "Fossengen and his people have done just such thinking. I believe we can expect to see more of him."

120

"I agree," Steve said. "And I don't think there's any question it was Fossengen's group that killed Major Ryland."

"Killed Ryland?"

Steve related the events that had taken place at Norton Air Force Base. Viejo shook his head. "If they would go so far as to assassinate an American officer in his own country . . ."

Mueller took over. "Colonel Viejo, I believe we had better brief Dr. Yavari and his daughter, as well as Jennings and Dr. Wells."

"A question before we talk with them," Steve said. "From what I understand, the high country around here . . . this plateau, the area around Temple Mountain and El Misti, all of this is considered sacred ground by the local natives?"

Viejo nodded.

"Then where did those natives come from?" Mueller asked. "The ones that tried to hit us at the airfield?"

"I expect they were brought here from the far north with the promise of much gold or other payment. They would not believe the local superstitions."

"And no one around here could identify them either," Steve added. "Fossengen seems to know what he's doing."

They shared a meal in the cabin of the C-47. Having certainly not expected a woman on this expedition, Steve found himself even more unprepared for Carla's effect on him. Her dark hair rested casually about her shoulders in the refuge of the airplane cabin, whereas outside it had blown wildly. Now, in the soft glow of the lamps, he could also study her lovely features. Their conversation in the cabin, shared with the others, was of the roadway, the mixture of huge stones and smaller rocks that could be seen, barely, beneath the glasslike surface material. As Viejo had said, she had grown up, literally, on studies of Peru's ancient past, and like Dr. Yavari had carried on the search to unlock the mysteries of an ancient

121

people that had built a civilization still defying today's science. Carla was separated from other women by more than her knowledge; she was a living thread from this ancient past to the present.

That night, when Carla was to be assigned her stand at guard, Steve made certain they would be together for those few hours. Outside the airplane and the small collection of tents, both of them in heavy, warm clothing, rifles slung to their backs, they walked slowly about the perimeter of the camp, careful to remain fairly close to the ghostlike airplanes in the mists. She *was* friendly to him; in the few minutes of conversation inside the C-47 cabin, she had made that evident. But he was hardly confident that it was especially personal. Perhaps even more to Carla than her father, because it was of her generation, the exploration of the moon was related directly to what they explored here in the dim past of their own people. There was that link, bond, between them.

Except he wanted Carla Yavari to know him as someone beside a man who had journeyed between worlds. He wanted her to know him as a . . . He looked at her in the mists of the bitterly uncomfortable night and decided it would be an advantage that they'd have plenty of time before he tried to get close . . . before she discovered he was steel and plastic as well as flesh and blood.

CHAPTER XIII

By MORNING the lower mists were gone, banished by a changing wind and the rising sun. Dr. Jennings and Dr. Yavari met with Steve inside a tent, the charts of the area spread out before them. Where to go next was their problem.

"We could search forever," Yavari said. "It would do no good. You see? Here?" His finger brushed the chart before him. "Valleys. Very deep. But a long time ago not a valley here. You understand? Earth tremors. Eruptions. Everything very much changed."

Jennings nodded. "We're all agreed, though, that our search area should lie between where we are and the volcano. It narrows somewhat where we must look to—"

"Dr. Jennings," Steve broke in, "what you're talking about is impossible. You know what this area is like?" He tapped the

123

charts where the valley was indicated. "Have you ever tried to fight your way through this stuff? We'd have to just about chew and tear our way through. That would be rough enough if we were trying to get from one point to another, but to carry out a *search?*"

"Then we must find a way of narrowing the search. The small airplane," he said suddenly. "We can use it to study the area—fly low over the general area between here and El Misti and—"

"Do you know what it's like out there?" Steve demanded.

"You mean the winds, I suppose."

"Yeah, doc, the winds. Here on the plateau they're doing a steady thirty knots and gusting to forty or fifty. And that's not the half of it. There's the turbulence . . . the chop we'll get off that range north of here, to say nothing of the downdrafts."

"I'm not frightened."

"You should be," Steve said, "because *I* am."

Yavari seemed excited. "It's a good idea. Before, on other flights, clouds made observation impossible. Today there are only high clouds. A very good break for us."

Jennings knew this high country well. Today *was* a relatively good day for aerial observation. Steve knew it. It was *possible* to fly, but he didn't like it. Whoever went along would quickly find out why. He left the tent to find Viejo and persuade him to let him do the flying in the Courier.

Rudy Wells declined the offer to make the flight. A look at the clouds streaming from the distant peaks and the intensity of the winds here on the plateau decided him against getting any farther from the ground than where his feet stood. Jennings and Yavari and Carla announced they would fly with him. Steve protested. They had no way of knowing what it was going to be like up there. Carla was at least young and strong, but her father and Jennings were . . . He gave it up and went to ready the Courier.

He checked out the airplane, personally checked to see that Jennings and Yavari were securely belted in the back seats, and ordered Carla to secure both seat belt and shoulder harness in the seat next to him. "No," she said. "I need to use this." She held up a 35-mm camera. "Especially made up for us," she said, smiling at him. "A Polaroid filmpack so that when we land we'll have the pictures we need."

"The harness or you stay on the ground," Steve told her.

For a moment it was a standoff. Outside the plane the others were aware of the obvious confrontation. Gusts rocked the Courier even with the tiedowns still secured. Carla looked coolly at the man with her, then secured the shoulder harness.

"It's an inertial reel system," Steve began, and got no further.

"I *know* what it is," she told him, looking straight ahead. "We are wasting time."

Carla Yavari, he hardly needed telling, was accustomed to her own way. Well not, he decided, in any airplane he flew. He signaled to the others he was ready to start. Viejo gave him the all-clear signal. The turbine ground into life, whined with its steady rising pitch. He watched the fuel pressure and flow and temperatures. She was alive. He signaled for them to pull the chocks and release the ropes. Again they signaled all clear, but remained by the wings as he ran through the quick checklist. They wouldn't need to taxi much today. Not with this wind. He waved to the men to clear away from the airplane, watched the marker flags whipping in the wind. He went to full power, the prop a thin blur before them, kept the stick full back as he released the brakes. The Helio rumbled forward, the wings trembling as they bounced along the grass. Almost as quickly as they started rolling she was fighting to break free of the ground. He held the stick back hard, full elevator deflection, and suddenly they were in the air and he was fighting her in the savage chop barely a hundred feet off the plateau. They

125

took off to the west; he decided to take advantage of the stiff winds and climb out at once to the north toward El Misti.

But even this short distance above the plateau the west wind they had on the surface vanished and the gales howled at them from the north. The left wing snapped down before a violent gust, and all in one moment the camera went flying from Carla's hands, her body snapped forward—caught by the inertial harness before her face could hit the panel—and the Courier was blown violently to the south, following that dropped wing.

They were flying but they didn't yet have the speed Steve needed to overcome the severity of the turbulence, and they were getting gust stalls that momentarily made the Helio shudder throughout its wings and fuselage. He heard a gasp from behind him as one of the two men was slammed against the side of the cabin. Steve had the nose *down,* not up as everyone else expected, and their speed picked up with a frightening rush as they combined their own speed over the ground with the winds that must have been sixty or seventy knots battering at them from out of the north.

Still, he needed more *air*speed. There was a sickening view of the south edge of Chalhuanca Plateau, barely fifty feet beneath them, trees and grass and brush startlingly clear as they crossed the edge of the plateau and plunged toward the distant valley. It was the only way to move and Steve took it, wrestling the controls to keep the wings basically level until the airspeed indicator began to crawl around its dial. Before them the Sicuani River snaked through the valley, and he took it as his eyeball reference. By the time they reached that point, he'd have to break out of the plunging river of air in which they hurtled forward and—

The snaking ribbon through green reached toward them faster than he'd expected. He had just enough time to shout to them above the roar of the wind and the rattling and banging sounds of the airplane. "Hang on," he yelled. "It's going to be rough coming out of this."

He glanced at Carla next to him. For the moment she'd given up trying to find the camera and was snugged against the backrest of her seat. A trickle of blood came from her lower lip.

He brought in full power and began the steady backpressure on the stick to get them out. The nose came up, but they were still descending, and he had no choice but to bring the Helio into a turn; as much as he didn't want to overload those wings at this moment, there really wasn't any choice. He felt the Helio fighting, and this time he was better prepared for the sudden shift when they jerked free of the downdraft. The Helio shot upward as if hurled away from a catapult. He didn't know how many g's they pulled coming out of it as the airplane soared wildly—the rate-of-climb indicator hugging the stop on the dial—but it was bad enough to scrunch neckbones, and he knew the other people with him were being punished, especially those in the back seat. And then they were out of it, the air still choppy, smacking them with sudden jolts, but the kind of ride the Helio could move through reasonably well.

He took a deep breath and turned to Carla, worried about that blood he'd seen. He figured it was from biting her lip. As he looked at her, she motioned with her head to her father and Jennings in the back seat. Steve turned. Jennings was a pasty white, his eyes half-closed. "The oxygen," Steve told her quickly. "Behind the front seats. Get masks on both of them." When she had the masks secured he reached to the oxygen console overhead and gave them 100 percent flow. "Now yourself," he said, "and one for me." She did as she was told. Moments later they were all feeling considerably better. Steve reduced the flow to demand and decided to leave the masks in place.

127

Carla looked ahead, saw El Misti looming high into clouds that obscured the peak. Her voice came lightly muffled by the thin plastirubber mask. "Well," she announced, "you warned us. I suppose one should apologize."

His smile was hidden by the mask. "You'd better do something about your lip," he told her, and saw the question in her eyes. "Your lip," he repeated. "You must have bitten yourself."

She felt with her hand beneath the mask, drew out her fingers with blood on them. "I didn't know," she said, barely loud enough for him to hear. She reached for a handkerchief in a pocket, dabbed, then gasped as a severe jolt slammed the Helio to one side.

Steve glanced behind, pointed ahead and down. "It gets rougher down there," he told her. "Better find your camera." She turned to her father and Jennings, who found the camera on the floor by their feet. They'd never noticed, during the sudden shocks after takeoff, that the camera had sailed back and dropped between them.

Steve flew northward. Their speed across the ground was barely fifty miles an hour, if that. From the rugged slopes of El Misti and the range bunched to each side of the volcano, a powerful river of air swirled across and downward to the valley over which they flew. Even beneath the thick clouds covering the upper peaks, Steve was able to make out violence of another and older nature well below them. Not even the thick forests could obscure the tumbling of the land, the great heaped blocks and piles tossed about by past quakes and volcanic eruption. Sheer walls fell away from gentle slopes, testifying to centuries past when this entire range must have suffered from the ubiquitous writhing of the earth. The dark remnants of old volcanic flow still covered many slopes. Steve found a strange familiarity between what he saw and the devastation in the country surrounding Flagstaff, Arizona, along the edge of the Painted Desert. Only this was on a far

128

grander scale and the chaos strewn downward from the higher peaks had managed to contribute its own ugly brand.

He needed to get between El Misti and Temple Mountain to its south. Easier said than done. They had moments of quiet air, grateful for the release from the constant pounding against their bodies. Jennings had already been sick twice, doing his best to avoid bothering the pilot, but nausea and vomiting in an airplane flying a berserk pattern through air as rough as the worst river rapids could hardly be concealed. After the second time Steve announced he was returning to the plateau, but he held to his course after the vehement objection of Jennings. The scientist angrily reminded Steve that no one had complained, that to quit now after what they'd gone through might lose them this same chance for weeks to come—or forever.

"Okay," he said, his tone masking his respect for Jennings and the others, too. "I'll keep this tin can in the air just so long as I think it's safe. But the moment it gets too hairy for me, which is when I think we may start bending metal, we go back. With no arguments." No one made any.

His only chance to get between El Misti and Temple Mountain was to get as low to the valley floor as was possible. A jumbled green carpet, thick and seemingly without bottom, loomed up at them as he dropped toward the valley jungle floor and wrestled with the controls. Carla gave up trying to take the pictures they wanted; she waited hopefully for a moment of calmer air. Steve wished her luck.

If he could get low enough there was a chance they would get beneath those invisible tumbling waterfalls of air pouring off the mountain ridges. There'd be almost a cushion beneath which he could scrape the tops of the trees—far better than staying in this cement mixer. And then the air calmed, miraculously it seemed. "You may not have much time," Steve told them quickly. "Make the most of it, Carla."

She went to work quickly with her camera as they rushed

129

over the tumbled jungle below. Steve made it through the wide, deep gorge lying between Temple Mountain and the volcano and was starting his turn to the south when Dr. Yavari leaned forward and spoke in Spanish to his daughter. Steve caught only fragments, but noticed Carla glancing quickly from her father to him. "He wants you to retrace the route we just flew," she said. "Can you, please?"

"What *for?*"

She tapped the camera. "From my side, Steve . . . I had to shoot across you for the pictures. There is something about Temple he wants to study later." Her eyes stressed the need.

He brought up the nose, the Helio leaping high, then sucked her around in a stall-turn that let them reverse course with the smallest turn possible. He paid no attention to them now, concentrating on his flying, as Carla leaned closer to her window, snapping pictures under her father's directions. Then they were out of the gorge, and fingers of turbulence were at them again.

"Now the south slope," he heard Carla say. He held back saying what was in his mind. They flew to the east until the stepped eastern slope of Temple Mountain was to his right. He came around in a wide turn, letting the wind carry them in a swooping rush until he was again flying west, but this time with Temple Mountain to his and Carla's right. Again the camera was busy. In the back seat Yavari had his face pressed against his window, ignoring the bumps of their flight, and Jennings was wedged in with him as both men pointed and exclaimed to one another.

"Wonderful," Jennings was shouting in Yavari's ear, pounding enthusiastically against his shoulder until another violent updraft weighed him heavily in his seat. Carla looked at him responsively. Steve didn't know what was going on, but he did know he had three happy people with him. He'd find out soon enough on the ground, because they quickly lost their

130

enthusiasm as he emerged from the protection of Temple Mountain and went staggering back into the violence they'd encountered right after takeoff.

If anything, it was worse now than when they'd first left the ground, and he knew it was going to take every ounce of skill he had to land. Bad enough in the air, but trying to bring this thing onto the ground without scattering it all over the plateau was another matter. He didn't want to show his concern to the others, but they must have known—he saw Carla turning to the men behind her, checking that they were secured by their belts, then snugging her own straps.

He came around to the Chalhuanca Plateau in a wide and flat turn, letting the wind do most of the work. One bit of luck was still with them. This far down from the range they were again catching the wind no more than ten or twenty degrees off their nose. He at least wouldn't have to fight a devilish crosswind. Ten or twenty degrees he could handle. It would have to be quick and dirty, no gentle approach ... a carrier technique. Get down low, slam her onto the ground, stick back in his gut and hold her down with power until the people waiting for them ran up to the plane and grabbed on tight.

He couldn't hold a decent approach. No way at all. He brought her around carefully, bringing in the first notch of flaps, trying to get her almost to walk on that surf-breaking air out there, but a draft sucked them downward and he was riding the power all the way, climbing back up that invisible slope, trying not to let the ship get away from him.

They slugged—good word for it—closer and closer to the final moment. The sheer face of the edge of the plateau loomed outward at them, shimmering in their own vision as they were banged and jerked about within the airplane. Then it flowed together with a wild rush. He found it critical one moment to crab wildly to compensate for the sudden crosswind, then kick away from the crab when the wind was on his nose. Power surges to fight the winds up and down, and they were coming down hard toward that tiny tiny strip. He saw the men watching as the tiny machine staggered down from the skies.

The grass loomed up at him. He flew her every inch of the way, snapping up a wing when wind slapped it down. They almost touched, swooped up, he brought her down, he *had* to commit. Then close again, he kept in the power on the edge of the stall, she was flying but sinking and he felt the tailwheel brush grass. Now. Forward on the stick, the gear coming in, *back fast* . . . hold her there, stick sucked back in his gut, plenty of power. Don't do anything else yet, just hold her. The wings trembled and wanted to get away from the ground again. He felt the sudden thud as two men threw themselves over the fuselage near the tail to hold it down with their weight, and he saw Wayne by the left wing, threading a rope through the tiedown slot, Mueller doing the same to the right. Hanging onto the ropes, Wells now with Mueller, Viejo with Wayne, they crab-walked the ship back to the parking area and tied her down. Finally he was able to kill the engine.

They sat inside the airplane, no one wanting to speak. Then Steve heard a quiet prayer in Spanish from Yavari. The men outside opened the doors and helped them out, Carla holding tight to the camera containing her precious pictures. They were led to the C-47 and went inside the cabin.

Only Viejo was left to go inside the Courier and secure any loose items, tie the sticks down with the seat belts. When he came from the airplane he stood in front of Steve, looking strangely at him. "I must speak to you later." Not another word. Not a question about the flight or what they might have found. Just that one sentence.

Steve turned to the Courier's cabin and looked inside. Then he understood. The throttle by the left cabin wall, on the quadrant. The throttle handle, in the shape of a steel sphere, easy for the left hand of the pilot to grasp while he held the stick in his right. But where Steve had held the throttle there was now only mangled steel. He held up his left hand, looked at the palm, and for the first time saw the little pieces of broken and jagged metal driven into the plastiskin.

He hadn't felt a thing.

Being *that* scared had overriden even bionics sensors.

How about that? In a way it was nice to be so scared. At least it was further proof he was more man than machine.

CHAPTER XIV

"BUT THERE'S no mistake, I tell you. We've gone over everything, studied it from a hundred different angles. This is almost surely the key people have searched for . . . for God knows how many years!" Dr. Jennings drew in air, forcing himself to return to the level of calmness demanded by Rudy Wells, but his eyes were intense and the lines of his face taut as he presented his argument to Steve Austin and Colonel Simon Viejo. By his side in the big tent were Dr. Yavari and Carla. The others, Wayne and Mueller, listened as observers.

Jennings' forefinger stabbed again at the chart. "Even when it was just a hint we were on the right track, although we didn't realize it. Then when we studied the magnetic heading of the crossroads, *and* the angle of structure of Temple Mountain . . ." He sat back, glancing at Wells, expecting the warning

135

he knew he deserved. But Rudy was silent, Jennings was learning how to pace himself and his body was adapting well to the thin air.

Carla leaned forward to reach the map. "What Dr. Jennings and my father are trying to convince you of," she said, "is that all we have seen points to Temple Mountain as our goal. You see"—she spread out the photographs—"Dr. Jennings first suspected that the Caya built their roadway structures along the cardinal points of the compass. If the crossroad is any indication, then his suspicions are certainly founded. If we take into consideration alterations in the magnetic field locally because of volcanic activity . . ."

Her intensity filled the tent; she commanded the moment. Her father nodded as she went through each point, was content to let her be his spokesman. It had become obvious to everyone that Yavari and his daughter had worked as a team so closely knit that each knew the other's thoughts.

"Do you understand, then?" she said to Viejo. "We *must* get to Temple Mountain. As quickly as possible. Everything we have seen, everything we have studied and examined points to Temple Mountain. It is our . . ."

"Lodestone?" Steve offered.

"Exactly." She smiled at Steve in appreciation.

The sound of the wind crowded into the tent with them. They were bundled in cold-weather clothing, and grateful for the heat from the two propane lamps glowing brightly on each side of the tent. The sides and roof of the tent billowed and sang from the outside pressures. It was as if they had been cut off from the rest of the world, prey for the siren call that Carla was bringing them with the image of Temple Mountain and its promise.

Colonel Viejo was an old hand at resisting siren calls. He knew the treachery of the back mountain country, remembered the men who had failed to come back from what they had rushed into so enthusiastically. "You wish to go to Temple Mountain?"

"Wish? We *must* go there," Carla said. "Everything we have learned points to it."

Viejo waved a hand to cut short the onslaught. "How do you propose we get from here, on this plateau, to there?"

"Why, the same way we got here, of course," Dr. Jennings said. "The way Steve and the others brought in our plane. They flew over the plateau, dropped in by parachute and . . ."

Steve shook his head. "The wind, Dr. Jennings. Anybody who bailed out into this wind wouldn't have a prayer of making it safely to the ground. Not with those rocks out there."

"Besides," Wayne added, "there isn't enough room for a strip. Maybe for the Helio, but you'd have to work at it awhile. Weeks, maybe."

"The weather," Dr. Yavari said with hope in his voice. "Maybe the weather will improve soon?"

"Do not count on it, doctor," Viejo said. "We are coming into September. You know what happens. The clouds are here most of the time, but the wind is here all the time. Worse in the months to come. Forget wings and parachutes."

"Then there is only one way," Carla said. "We must walk."

A groan came from Rudy Wells. "I was afraid someone might get that idea." He looked at Carla and shook his head. *"Walk?"*

Viejo had waited. "Miss Yavari," he said, "do you know what that jungle valley is like?"

"Of course I know. I know my country as well as—"

"You do not know *this* country," Viejo said. "Unless you have, yourself, been there, you do not know. Nothing compares with it."

"Colonel, we came here looking for something," Steve said. "Dr. Jennings tells us Temple Mountain is where we may find what we're after. We're going."

"Colonel," Carla said quietly to Viejo, "you will not stop us, will you?"

Viejo stared ahead, seemed to evade her question.

Dr. Yavari leaned forward, addressing Colonel Viejo in Spanish, but Viejo answered in English. "During the day I tried to reach the Ayabaca airport. By radio from the C-47. That way I could get word to my headquarters, ask for more men." He shook his head. "Impossible. In any case, it might have taken them days or a week to get here. With the weather over those mountains—"

Carla again, her voice pleasant but insistent. "You have not answered me, colonel."

"Why *this* mountain?" demanded Viejo. "How do you know *this* is the mountain?"

"Colonel Viejo, I owe you an apology," Yavari said in a tone that took them all by surprise. "We have been foolish. Of course, how could you have known?"

Carla stepped in. "What we know as Temple Mountain," she said, "was so named because of its unusual shape. The steep, inwardly sloping walls always seemed to have a strange character to them, as if nature had grown from its rock a temple. Colonel Viejo, it has been right before our eyes all this time. The upper ramparts of the mountain . . . we believe it is a temple, not simply shaped like a temple. The high section, the high seven or eight hundred feet, colonel, is the temple we have been seeking."

"You mean the temple rests on top of the mountain?"

"No, we believe the peak is not the mountain. We believe the peak was built . . . by the Caya. You can surely understand, Colonel Viejo, that my father and I feel literally a magnetic pull from that place that was built by our ancestors."

138

It took them one full day to work their way down from the Chalhuanca Plateau. One full day of lurching, stumbling progress, the undergrowth thickening with every mile down.

They left the Chalhuanca at first sign of light the morning after their confrontation in the tent. The temperature rose with every hour. The sun broke through intermittently as broken clouds swept high over them, adding to the heat of the day, but not as much as their decreasing elevation.

They had expected fairly easy going. They were still strong and the air pressure went up as the height went down, but the surface underfoot was treacherous. Lava rock beneath the tropical growth crumbled easily. Scraped skin became a common ailment, and everyone took special care to avoid a sprained ankle. As the temperature rose they began to remove their outer clothing, bulk and weight they would gladly have thrown away except that they knew its urgent need when they began to work their way up the flanks of Temple Mountain.

The heavy rains of previous days had turned much of the ground into a treacherous bog that became evident only when their feet went through the leafy growth underfoot and they discovered the effort needed simply to lift one foot after the other. Years of sifting leaves and natural debris, and the rain washing down the looser soil from the slopes of the Chalhuanca, turned other large areas into this same energy-sapping muck, a substratum thick enough to lay in the hand but unable to support their weight. This mess was worsened by the heavy growth all about them that had to be slashed with machete.

Steve, Viejo, Mueller alternated as point, trying to help Jennings and Yavari in their progress by making footfalls for them—so that they could step where the leaders had walked. It worsened the problem, for any foot pressure brought the water closer to the surface, and the weight of two people in one place meant sinking deeper into the muck. It went slowly,

139

enervatingly, and Temple Mountain, lying now just east of north, seemed farther and farther away.

Viejo took breaks every ninety minutes, not so much for himself as for the others, who were still too fired by the promise of what lay before them to pace themselves properly. He watched them for signs of weakness, overexertion, and as the hours went by he kept looking more and more at Steve Austin. To Viejo's skilled eye the American was actually disturbing. After seeing him slash aside vines and creepers and heavy growth with a machete that seemed possessed of its own strength, he recalled the Helio Courier and the throttle quadrant crushed to metal pulp. He said nothing, though he noted that it was when Steve Austin took the lead, cutting a path for the rest of them, that they made their best time.

And then it was time to quit for the first day, except where to spend the night? Underfoot it was still damp, but trees lifted massive roots from the muck to form shelflike upthrusts, and the roots themselves were covered with an orange moss that was springy and yielding. With their bedrolls well secured they would be safe here for the night. After dinner eaten from cans, Viejo made sure they were wedged in properly. Then he went twenty yards from where they were clustered and from a tree branch he hung a small but powerful light. Then another light fifty yards from the first. The others wondered about this, but not for long. As night enveloped them the lights were inundated by swarms of insects of extraordinary size and variety—most of which would otherwise have chosen them for company.

"Your netting, everyone. Use it generously," Viejo told them.

Wayne gestured at the lights. "They seem to be doing a pretty good job, colonel. Looks like we won't need the nets."

"What about the *manta blanca?*" Rudy said. "Not to mention the things that crawl on you."

"*Manta blanca?* What's that, doc?"

"You'll see. It means white blanket."

"Blanket?"

He found out soon enough, and by then he was wrapping himself furiously in his netting and burrowing within his bedroll. The *manta blanca* was there, all right—a white blanket of small, aggressive, persistent gnats. So many they seemed to be a fog in the air, and found the chemicals and odors of the living bodies far more attractive than the lights.

It was a rotten night.

The morning was little better. They awoke to find their netting and bedrolls—and themselves—covered with hundreds of small green, gold-striped tree frogs. They were everywhere, staring at them before their noses, swarming on their equipment, not readily discouraged by sound or movement. Despite their unwelcome guests, Viejo insisted on a full breakfast of rations before they broke camp.

To their relief they worked out of the tangled matting by early afternoon. Their altitude was thousands of feet lower than it had been on the Chalhuanca, but they were still more than eight thousand feet above sea level and the constant energy drain on their bodies brought weariness through muscles and bone. It was with enormous relief that they saw before them several miles of relatively clear ground. But this was still almost unknown jungle or grassy country at high altitude. They had moved no more than a hundred yards into the grass when they discovered that the edges of the high grass were saw-toothed like knives, and slashed as badly. Bloody nicks and cuts stopped them. The men hacked out a clearing to rest while they considered their latest obstacle.

The machetes proved wearying to the strongest of them—the rubbery grass fibers blunted the whistling metal. More even than the thick jungle, the high grass fields were draining away their energy. Again they broke their trail,

141

looking back on the snakelike path they had hacked to get this far, falling exhausted, their bodies soaked with sweat and chilled almost as quickly by the thin, still-cold air about them.

In these Peruvian highlands insects—especially huge moths and butterflies—had an incredible scent, and liking for salt, which now lay thick, caked and inviting, on their skins and embedded in their clothing. The fluttering winged creatures came in hordes, brought unerringly to their presence by the scent of salt on the unceasing winds. Netting about their faces kept the buzzing insects from clogging their mouths and noses and ears, but they knew that staying here could be their undoing. They were huddled together in their misery, and Steve knew that what the jungle had failed to do, the tall cutting grass and insects could accomplish—destroy their hope of being able to go on. He wrapped netting about himself, honed his machete and decided it was time to take chances. Viejo already suspected something, as perhaps did some of the others. So—

He stepped forward, the machete clamped in his bionics fist. No longer did he hold back, measuring the swings so they would appear normal, or shifting from his bionics limb to his right, natural arm. The bionics arm became what it had been designed to be—an instrument of enormous strength and durability. The machete slashed from left to right, a near blur. Grass flew in a cloud of its own as Steve started moving and never slackened his pace. The others—all except Rudy Wells, who now most especially understood why Goldman had insisted Steve Austin take this mission—merely stared into a blizzard of grass cuttings.

Dr. Yavari shook his head in disbelief, turned to the only man in their group who seemed unimpressed by what was happening. "Doctor Wells . . . ?"

"I'm going to ask all of you a favor," Rudy said. "Don't ask

142

me any further questions because I know the answers. And whatever happens, please do not ask *him.*"

They stared after Steve, already more than two hundred yards ahead of them, moving at a seemingly inexorable pace. No one spoke. They picked up their gear, almost able to ignore the clouds of insects about them, and began to follow in a long broken line. Rudy Wells brought up the rear of the procession. They marched for another hour as Steve slashed a way through the grass that had threatened to choke off their hopes. For a while Carla stayed close to Steve, studying the man as he went through his incredible performance. At first she had thought his slashing labors were effortless, but as she caught a side view of his body she saw the perspiration staining his clothing, the gleam of wetness on his face. He was soaked through. She managed a closer look, caught her breath as she saw the telltale signs of red along the side of his face and his neck. Saw-toothed grass edges slashed by the machete were tiny razors; as they flew or were tossed back by the wind they took nicks of skin from his face and neck. He at least bleeds, Carla thought, wondering all the more as he fought through the stubborn defenses of the high plateau. Carla edged back slowly through the group until finally she was with Rudy. For a while she walked with him, silent, glancing at him. Finally, she had to ask.

"Dr. Wells . . ."

He understood her question, of course. He would have to ask her to take it on faith that for now there could be no answer.

CHAPTER XV

~~~~~~

ON THE fourth day they thought Aaron Mueller would die.

They were a day or two from Temple Mountain. Their rations were starting to run low, and Viejo worried about their condition if they should be caught without food. Small, two-toed deer had eluded them for two days running, until Viejo finally managed to flush one of the animals. Rudy Wells snapped two quick shots, one to the neck and the other to the head. Fresh, fire-roasted meat helped return their spirits, and Viejo consented to a longer break than he would ordinarily have permitted. They barely finished their meal in time; the late afternoon brought with darkening skies and lowering temperatures a cruel storm. The rain continued without let-up for hours, soaking them in their makeshift camp, turning the ground beneath into a quagmire. And then the hail began.

Hailstones the size of marbles at first, growing larger and larger, until in desperation they burrowed beneath their packs and equipment to keep from being pounded to death. It was the first time, as they scurried to escape the rocky barrage, that Carla Yavari found herself alone with Steve. No time to look for her father. Steve made a protecting mound of their gear and they huddled together, she in his arms, as the storm raged about them and the world went crazy with icy shrapnel from the heavens. She was asleep, exhausted physically and emotionally, when the hailstorm finally passed them by. They did not move for the rest of the night.

In the morning their goal was a succession of ledges that formed the beginning of the upslope leading directly to Temple Mountain. From this point on the going would be slower, although their morale was improved by the sight of their objective so close before them.

Steve looked them over. None would have survived the journey if the distance had been greater. Their clothing, his included, was torn and in many places already rotted from the combination of use, dampness, and tearing by grass and foliage. Boots were shreds, held together with tape and rope. The men had not shaved—except for Viejo, who would, it seemed, take the time and effort on a journey to hell itself. They suffered from skin rot, chafing, and only the careful ministrations of Rudy Wells had prevented outbreaks of worse disorders that could have crippled them. Steve looked forward to the higher altitude of the mountain. They were welted from insect bites as well as their other sores, and they would find some relief in the colder temperatures of higher altitude, where they would also leave behind the tiny winged and crawling creatures that had made such a misery of their lives these past days.

So the ledges, despite the increased drain on their physical resources, were a welcome objective—signaling also the beginning of the end of their enervating trek through the high jungle valley. Aaron Mueller had taken the lead. He was still one of the strongest in the group, determined to push on just so long as the others were able to stay with him. He had worked his way up the first ledge, secured a knotted line to a boulder and dropped it down to the others. A wise move. One man would follow Mueller, and the two on top of any steep ledge could haul up the supplies and heavy packs to enable the others to climb without such encumbrance.

Mueller gained a shelf perhaps three hundred feet above them, a fairly steep slope but one that promised fairly easy access to the others. Rudy Wells was just starting after him, using the knotted rope both as a guide and a climbing assist, when they heard a sound that stopped them cold in their tracks—a high-pitched, furious buzz saw unlike any they'd ever known. Except Viejo and Yavari, who looked up the slope toward Mueller. Now it was clear to the others this was where the sound came from. Viejo had brought his hands, cupped, to his mouth to shout a warning when Mueller's scream broke the morning air. They froze, saw Mueller now close to the edge, flailing his arms, still screaming.

"Austin!" Viejo tossed a smoke grenade to him. "Get up there quickly and use this!"

Steve shed his pack and slipped the grenade inside his shirt. He took the first sloping edge of the wall in a rush, his bionics legs pounding dirt and rock behind him. Then the rope, grasping it, running, climbing, pulling as he went up the steep rock wall. He paused only a moment at the edge, and from below they now saw the bright-orange smoke being spewed out under pressure and Steve disappearing over the edge to where Mueller must have fallen.

"Doctor Wells, quickly," Viejo said. "Your medical kit. Take nothing else but get up there at once." Rudy was out of his pack, securing the kit to his body straps and starting up the

147

slope. He climbed, scratching and bruising himself. Steve leaned over the edge.

"Doc, get a grip on the rope and hang on!"

Rudy gasped for air, clutched the rope with both hands, his feet twined beneath him, and felt himself jerked away from the side of the slope. He swung wildly in the air, was hauled upward like a fish on a line as Steve pulled him in. Then he was there, Steve helping him to get his balance.

"My God, what in the name of . . ."

Steve held out his hand—the left one, Rudy noticed gratefully. In the palm, a small wasp, its afterbody a fluorescent, dazzling green. "There must have been fifty of them," Steve said. "He's crazy with the pain."

Rudy pushed past Steve, knelt by the man twisted in agony. The wasp stings weren't puffy as Rudy had expected. Where the barbs had stabbed, the skin was white with a tiny bright-red center. Rudy spoke to Mueller as he groped in his kit.

"Aaron, can you hear me?" No answer. Rudy found what he was looking for. He'd need several shots of this if they were going to save him. Mueller flailed about like a man drowning.

"Hold him," Rudy ordered, as the first needle went into the chest near the heart. Mueller cried out again, not from the needle. "He's going through more hell than even you can imagine," Rudy said as he readied a second injection, this into the arm. "He feels like he's on fire, and as far as his nerves are concerned, *he is*. He's burning alive and—damn it, tighter, Steve."

"He acts like he's blind, doc."

"He is." Steve looked hard at Rudy. "If he comes out of this, he'll get his sight back. If he doesn't, he—"

Mueller twisted, arching his back. Steve clamped tight, and Mueller slumped unconscious.

"Steve, I'm winded. Quick . . . mouth-to-mouth resuscitation."

Steve bent to him, quickly readying Mueller and putting his mouth over that of the unconscious man. Rudy was leaning all his weight on Mueller's chest, trying to apply a steady pressure beat to the heart. He kept it up for a minute, then leaned over and put his ear to Mueller's chest. He tapped Steve on the shoulder and fell back, exhausted.

"He's got good heart action," Rudy gasped. "He's breathing now."

Steve slumped against a rock. "Nothing else to do?"

Rudy shook his head, forcing himself to breathe in long, deep draughts of air. He was white, but Steve noticed the color returning slowly. For a few minutes Rudy didn't answer, trying to get back his wind. "Better tell them down there," he gestured, weakly, "that Mueller's probably going to make it."

Steve called down and tossed over the knotted line. Viejo was soon with them. He studied Mueller for a moment, turned to Steve, who showed him the dead wasp. "A shame, to lose a man like that . . . ."

"What the hell do you mean?"

"That thing"—Viejo pointed to the wasp—"nobody can survive an attack by a swarm of those. I see on his face and neck where they struck. The poison stops the heart, freezes the lungs and muscles."

"I don't think so this time," Rudy said. "He's going to make it."

Viejo looked from Wells to Mueller. "It has never happened before. I am very sorry . . . ."

"Well, look again."

Viejo couldn't believe it—Mueller stirred. Steve helped him to a sitting position. Mueller blinked his eyes, trying to focus. Viejo hurried to him, staring intently. "Impossible . . . but, I see him alive!" Then, to Rudy Wells: "How?"

Rudy pointed to the kit. "Something new," he said quietly. "We developed it as an antidote to nerve gas, includes atropine. We never tried it on a human before, but it's worked on test animals." He glanced at Mueller, who was fully alert now, listening. "I only brought it along because of certain eels you have in your rivers that paralyze with their sting or bite. This medicine is the only known antidote for that eel ... damned lucky for our friend here that it works against wasp stings, too."

Viejo had turned back to Mueller, who was climbing to his feet, hardly able to believe his own recovery. Viejo extended his hand to clasp Mueller's. "Tell me," Viejo said, "how it feels to come back from the dead."

The rest of the ascent was slow, grueling, bone-wearying. As they climbed higher along the western escarpment, the broad base of which led finally to the suddenly rising flanks of the monolith shape of Temple Mountain, they kept moving into constantly thinning air. They expected this, of course, but their weariness came close to bringing them down. Coordination was faulty in pulled and stinging muscles. The lack of enough oxygen did more than exhaust them, it interfered with normal clear thinking. At times one or more would stop, head spinning, spots before eyes. They were dangerously close to breaking down. Little argument, though, about continuing. Who could argue it now, with their goal so visible, looming into the sky? For that matter, they lacked the strength for a real argument of any kind.

On a high ledge, with comfortable grass and moss about them, huge boulders providing excellent windbreaks, Rudy Wells called a halt for the day. The others needed no prompting to slide gratefully to the ground. With rest and Rudy's massive vitamin doses they could at least partially recharge themselves.

Rudy went to Steve. "We've got to make a camp of this place," he told him. "These people must pull themselves together. All of them. Viejo's adapted to the altitude but he's strangely withdrawn and—"

"What Viejo needs," Steve interrupted, "is responsibility. He isn't in charge of this group, Rudy. He can't function with a loose crowd like this. He knows they need him but he's afraid to overstep his bounds. I suppose I could do it, but Viejo should be the one."

Rudy glanced at the Peruvian officer, sitting alone on a rock ledge, staring into the distance. "What do I do?" Rudy asked Steve.

"Go to him and ask for help. Put him in charge. Even you, doc. Take *his* orders."

"And you?"

"Never mind, just try it."

Wells turned and walked slowly to Viejo. Steve saw them talking. Viejo shrugged, and it was clear even from a distance that Rudy was losing his temper. Viejo got to his feet and came face to face with the American. More argument, and then Viejo turned aside—not away from the doctor, but to stare at the jungle floor far below them. He talked again with Rudy, pointing. Moments later he had his binoculars to his eyes and was scanning an area in the distance. He lowered the glasses slowly, handed them to Wells. As the doctor sought what Viejo had seen, the latter turned from him and went to the other members of the expedition sprawled listlessly among their packs.

Steve was pleased. Viejo was like a man with new life, showing the authority the others needed. There were curses from Phil Wayne. Weary to the bone, short-tempered, he was spoiling for any kind of fight. Steve got to his feet, his pack over one shoulder, and walked slowly in front of Wayne and Viejo. On the lee side of a high boulder, Steve began to set up a small tent. Viejo had watched every move, and the Peruvian was sharp enough to know the American was setting himself up as an example. If Steve Austin could take orders from Colonel Viejo—although only Austin and Viejo knew no words had passed between them—there could hardly be argument from anyone else.

It began to take shape. Windbreak shelters and tents. Carla helping her father and Dr. Jennings, and then retiring to her own small tent. Razors were broken out, even if it meant shaving with water that boiled so swiftly in the thin air it was almost tepid. Their small group came alive under the constant verbal sawing from Viejo.

"Steve?" Wells came into the tent, sat on the ground with his legs crossed beneath him. He gestured to take in the others. "Good idea. It's working."

Steve nodded. "Trick is to keep it going."

"That won't be any problem."

"Oh?"

"Did you see Viejo looking over the valley with his binoculars? He found what he was looking for."

Steve's hands became motionless inside his pack. He waited.

"Company," the doctor said.

Steve eased himself to the ground. "Sooner than I thought. How far away?"

"The colonel says at their present rate, one to two days. If they really press, maybe eighteen hours."

"They can't get here before dawn tomorrow and they won't show in daylight. It's tomorrow night at the earliest. That at least gives us a little time to arrange a reception committee."

The word had now reached them all about the sighting of the group no more than a day's steady travel away. It had to be Fossengen and his men. Viejo cursed softly. "If only I could have reached Ayabaca by radio," he said, "then *our* men would be trailing Mr. Fossengen."

152

They began preparations for their reception committee. They were agreed it would be a mistake to give in to the temptation to engage in a showdown struggle with the group now closing in on them. They had no idea of the numbers involved, although Viejo was convinced it would be an efficient party. "Mercenaries," he said. "Fossengen has Julio Ruperez with him. That's how he controls the natives they brought here from the north. They are frightened of Ruperez. We have been waiting a long time to attend to that one. He has a hold on them. Their families. They are kept in a small village and guarded well. If a man deserts Ruperez, he knows his family will be butchered."

"And he gets away with it?"

"As in your country, one must have proof before . . . Still, if we prepare our reception with special taste, we may eliminate the problem of Julio Ruperez. Think of all the money we will save if there is no need for a trial."

Steve stood up and pointed back along the trail they had made on the way to their present location. He gathered his pack and told Phil Wayne to pick up his gear and come with them. He turned to Mueller. "There's a chance they've got a scout or two ahead of them," Steve told him. "You'd better stay sharp. From now on keep a shell in the chamber *all* the time. Everybody."

Mueller nodded. "Anything else?"

"Take a good, careful look all around you. Put everything in relationship to everything else. Make a sketch of it. We might need it in the dark. If we know the layout well enough we're one up on them. In case."

CHAPTER XVI

~~~~~~

THEY STARTED with first light the next morning. Viejo had
them awake and packing their gear in the dark, and when the
still invisible sun began to cast a gray glow over their height,
they were ready to finish their tasks. Refreshed, filled with a
new sense of purpose, experienced at careful breathing in the
thin air, they moved upward along the gently sloping surface.
It was the sort of splendid morning that seemed to dismiss the
threat of the group trailing them. They were under way less
than an hour when the morning brightened swiftly. Heading
east, they walked directly into a spectacular sunrise. Breaks in
the clouds filled with golden and pink light as the sun slashed
its way through. And directly before them, rearing impossibly
high, was Temple Mountain, its flank washed in dazzling early
morning light.

For a moment they stopped, bringing binoculars to play on the massive south wall. The low angle of morning light could bring out features that might otherwise escape them. Along the steep slope, which they estimated at sixty to seventy degrees, they saw vines and creepers that had had thousands of years to work their way along the monolithic peak. And they saw something else.

"There's no mistake," Dr. Jennings said. "See the south edge? That's a sharp break. It's an *edge,* and it runs true for the whole height of . . ." He had started to say "mountain," but changed his mind and called it ". . . structure." Indeed it did seem artificial. A natural fault with so long an unbroken line? Impossible. Impossible? Looking through binoculars at a low sun angle is hardly scientific proof. They'd have to wait to be absolutely certain. It wouldn't be long.

It was exactly two hours and twenty minutes later. Their speculation proved conservative.

They stood at the base of what had been misnamed a mountain, for mountains are not made of massive blocks of stone fitted so perfectly they seem to have been welded together, the separation of one huge stone from another only a thin seam-line. It towered above them, a wide-based obelisk, a monolith, a man-made mountain of formed and fitted stone. Magnificent. Old beyond their calculation. Impossible? True.

They looked at one another in a daze. Tears were in Carla's eyes as she held her father's hand. Dr. Yavari leaned back, shaking his head in wonder. Steve looked at Colonel Viejo, saw the pride in his eyes, nodded to him. No question any longer. Here was the sign of an ancient civilization that superseded, that towered over, all they had ever discovered of the Inca or the Maya or the Aztec or any people, the sign of a people who had built in this high jungle land a monument that dwarfed the pyramids standing above the Egyptian desert.

Steve turned to Phil Wayne, his cameras already clicking,

156

Rudy Wells helping. Steve caught Mueller's eye, and the latter nodded. He took his rifle and binoculars and worked his way back along the trail, selecting a high hummock for a vantage point to study the land behind them.

Steve sensed how they felt. All of them, but especially the Peruvians. This was uniquely their moment, a sweep backward in time for so many thousands of years. He had felt something of the same thing himself when he first stepped out on the moon's dusty surface. He had stood in lifeless dust and looked back across a quarter-million miles of vacuum to see the home world of man, than stunning blue-white marble against velvety black.

Now these people were seeing a view of comparable sweep. Theirs was a view through time that stretched incomparably farther than anything of earth he had seen from the moon.

"I have seen this before." Dr. Yavari guided his fingertips across the face of the stone, the answering pressures telling him as much as might be learned by a blind man. "All my life I have looked for such things . . . stones . . . doorways . . . secret ways to enter." He glanced at the others, winced a moment as a flash from Wayne's camera caught him in the eyes. "It is a matter of knowing, the touch, where to place it. Then, as these people intended . . ." He stared at one huge face of stone, motioned to Jennings and to his daughter. Moments later, using his cap, Jennings was scrubbing furiously at the stone. Dust and leaves flew in all directions. Wherever he scrubbed, a bas-relief appeared.

They stared at symbols, drawings, figures. Yavari motioned for a floodlight to gain starker relief. He was lost to them as he leaned closer, peering intently. He spoke with little conscious awareness of his words, but Carla was by his side, writing furiously to get down what he said. Suddenly she turned to Steve and the others. "It is a strange form of language, to be

157

sure, but still it is not completely unknown." She gestured to where her father was standing, studying, brushing his fingers against the wall carvings. "There is a commonality to almost all the ancient languages," she went on. "Before, when we came across tribes that were unknown, it did not take long to interpret their messages. The general similarities are really a challenge of logic more than of translation."

"There don't seem to be any openings along this whole flank," Steve said. He turned. "Phil, get whatever you can on film, and be ready to pick up your gear to get inside when and if Dr. Yavari finds his opening." He turned again. "Rudy, you stay with them. Keep a shotgun eye on things." He pointed at Viejo. "Let's go."

"But—" Carla looked bewildered.

"It's Mueller," Steve said. "He's got company in sight." He tapped the small transceiver radio clipped to his shirt. "He's calling us." Without another word he took off at a dead run, Viejo following close behind. Carla stared after him, then turned back to her father.

Steve and Viejo crouched as they ran, staying as much as possible within the cover of boulders and brush. They came up to Mueller, who also had managed some concealment. He pointed down the path.

"At least ten," he said. "They're loaded. Pros, by the looks of it. They've got a point man out on each side, while the others are coming up slower behind them."

"How far from the camp?"

Mueller glanced at Viejo. "Another hundred yards, maybe less."

Viejo looked at Steve. "We wait?"

Steve nodded. "The scouts should miss the wire. That means the main body will be right behind them. When the explosives go, we aim for the scouts. Aaron, you work on the man on the right with me. Colonel?"

Viejo patted the rifle stock. "The left one is mine."

They settled themselves in and waited. Steve put the binoculars to his face and looked back toward the base of the great temple. Dr. Yavari had left the inscriptions on the stones and was sliding his hands over a smooth-faced rock.

Steve turned back. Through binoculars they watched their trackers working their way cautiously along the trail. Steve was sure he could now recognize Fossengen—the big man had stopped and was studying the area where they had camped. One of the scouts rose from a cluster of boulders and waved an all-clear signal.

"Keep coming," Mueller said, low to himself.

Fossengen obviously was an old hand. He sent two men ahead of his main group. The two scouts watched from their positions ahead of and to the sides of the main body.

The lead man of the two approaching the camp hit the trip wire concealed within brush. Instantly a half-dozen explosive charges buried just beneath the ground in loose rocks detonated. A bright orange flash erupted with a booming roar and both men were hurled crazily through the air. At almost the same instant Viejo's rifle sounded as he fired a short burst. A third man tumbled to the ground. Steve and Mueller fired together at the point man on the right. They weren't sure if they hit him, and there wasn't time to find out. The three of them turned and ran back toward the temple.

Only Rudy Wells was in sight, crouched by a high opening in the otherwise unbroken face of the temple wall. No need to ask. Yavari knew what he was doing. He'd found the place to apply pressure, and the great rock had moved. How many centuries had it stood in place here? And who were these people who had built so that not even this enormous span of time—that began before the western world saw its first agricultural settlements—would not destroy or at least make their handiwork useless? . . . They came to the opening. Steve pushed them through, followed the last man in. Phil Wayne had already turned on mercury-cell lamps. He played a bright light on the doorway, and Carla moved forward, her hand on an inscription carved in a rock, waiting.

"Close it," Steve urged. She pressed her fingers firmly against the inscription. A massive stone, taller than a man and nearly four feet wide, rumbled heavily as it swung on a pivot and sealed the entrance-way. The stone boomed into place with a dull echo. They stood quietly, listening to the sound drift along unknown passageways and chambers before it came back to them, rippling in hoarse whispers. Dust drifted across the lights, a dust of untold centuries.

Yavari looked around him, his eyes showing the awe he felt. Steve and Viejo looked at one another. Viejo nodded and Steve took a deep breath. "I know it's an intrusion," he said slowly, "but you must listen to me." He related what had happened, explaining the blast they had heard, the cracking sounds of the rifles. He also saw that the words had really failed to reach Dr. Yavari, and that Dr. Jennings was not far removed from the state of the Peruvian scientist. He looked sharply at Carla, saw the understanding in her eyes. What her father did not hear she would hear for him.

"Those people out there won't hold back anymore," Steve warned. "Mueller saw at least ten. We know we took care of three, but there could have been several more who stayed out of our sight. We're committed now. We had the lead, and they'll move slowly where we camped. But that's about all the slowing down we could manage. It's too bad we couldn't rig another welcome for them outside these walls, but there wasn't time."

"Steve, I don't think they can get in here," Phil Wayne said, speaking for the benefit of all of them. "I mean, unless Dr. Yavari had found that pressure release..." He shook his head. "We'd still be out there."

Steve stopped him. "It sounds good, Phil, but don't sell them short. There may be more than one way in here. We don't know. We didn't have time to look. And if Dr. Yavari could figure the way in through this stone—" He cut off his words and nodded to Viejo. The colonel motioned to Mueller, and both men went back to the stone that had moved to permit their entrance. There were loose blocks of stone lying about on the floor beneath them. They immediately started piling the blocks against the vertical stone to wedge it in place.

"Rudy, mark off where we are," Steve told the doctor. "Make it a clear mark, too. This place is probably filled with all kinds of corridors and passages, and we can get lost faster than it takes to think about it. Start numbering every cross-corridor we come to. Mark it where we can all see it. This could be a labyrinth. We've got to be able to find our way around when we start coming out again."

Steve turned to Yavari. "Doctor, you've been in temples like this before."

"Not like *this*." Yavari smiled. "There is nothing—"

"I know," Steve broke in quickly, "but a structure like this, it's like the pyramids, isn't it? The people who built it must have thought of looters—people who might come here to rob graves or strip it of its treasures, whatever they might be. So wouldn't they set up a system of deadfalls, traps?"

"You're right," Rudy Wells said. "It's the first complication we should watch for. If a true believer were to come in here—he wouldn't be in a rush. He'd take his time to examine, study, learn . . . he'd move slowly. If we don't do likewise we'll be vulnerable to . . . ." He let it hang.

"Understood. We need to be careful," Mueller said. "But where do we go?"

"If what Dr. Jennings and Rudy told us before is on the track," Steve said carefully, "we've got to work our way higher. We've got to climb. This entire structure is intended to make height important. It's a guess," he admitted, "but unless anyone has something better to offer . . ."

"I believe you are right," Carla said. "There is a strong association here, in what my father has already seen, that suggests heat and light. It is almost certainly sun-oriented. Which means"—she looked up as if she could see through the massive stone above them—"that way."

"Everybody pick up their gear," Steve ordered. "Rudy, you mark the way. Aaron, stay close to Dr. Yavari. Make sure he's got plenty of light. And if anybody sees anything that seems a problem, call out, and everybody else freeze where they are until we figure what's going on. Colonel Viejo?" The Peruvian officer looked at him. "Anything else?" Steve asked.

Viejo smiled briefly. "The words are yours," he said, "but the thoughts are exactly mine."

"Okay, then let's get with it," Steve said quietly as they started out along a corridor that took them further and further into dusty time.

"The floor is descending slowly." They stopped to watch Viejo, kneeling. He placed a bullet on the stone floor and watched it. The bullet rolled in the direction they were headed. Viejo took it up and rose to his feet. "You will find all the other corridors like this, I believe," he said. "It seems they knew what they were doing, the men who engineered this place."

Mueller showed the question on his face. "Any special reason?"

"I'd say it had to do with the problem of heavy rain in this country," Viejo said. "Condensation, too. The slopes guaranteed a water run. Likely there are exit points throughout the temple. And entrance points, perhaps . . ."

They resumed their slow progress. Steve studied a compass, shoved it back into a pocket. "Useless in here," he said. "It could be the stone, or something magnetic."

162

"We're walking northeast," Rudy said. "And I'll wager it's forty-five degrees. Remember? They built their roads on the cardinal points of the compass. We came into this place on the southwest corner. If it's one of the main passageways, it should lead to the center of the temple."

No one contested him. Carla had fashioned a face mask from a kerchief for her father, and the others soon followed her example. Dust lay heavy all about them, piled on the floor and clinging to the walls. Even with the slight breeze of their passage, the dust kicked up from the stone floor, sending irritating clouds swirling around them.

"The corridor's getting wider," Wayne announced. They stopped again, looked behind them, then forward again. Wayne was right.

"Look!" Dr. Jennings pointed with excitement. "Can you see it? There's some sort of light, a glow down there." He was right. The corridor ended, or seemed to end, in a dim bowl of light.

"It must be air," Yavari said. "You understand? They had no machinery as we know it to condition a building. So they designed openings at different places. This moves air."

The others nodded and continued their walk in silence. Their flashlights stabbed through the dust preceding them. Again they stopped. On the left wall of the corridor, the outline of a door. No handle or recession in the stone; more of the symbols they had seen at the entrance-way. "We could open it," Viejo said.

"Later. Let's first find out more about how this place is set up," Steve said. "Rudy, mark it, will you?" Wells wrote carefully on the stone wall by the thin outline of a doorway, using a marker pen from his kit.

Several more minutes of cautious movement passed, and they slowed down their steps. The light ahead was brighter now, and they saw clearly how right Dr. Yavari had been in his judgment. At the end of the corridor there was some kind of enormous chamber, but their vision was diffused by shafts of light stabbing through dust, making it seem as though they were looking into a fog.

Dr. Jennings moved ahead of the others to take up the lead. His face showed the excitement building in him. "This corridor leading to some main chamber ... what we're looking for ... it's got to be just ahead of us. A dome ... they usually built a dome in the center of their temples. It can't be that much different from the Inca or the Maya." He probed with his flashlight, began to walk faster, well ahead of the others now.

Steve had a premonition. Deadfalls ... traps for the unwary who rushed in without thought of what had been designed as protection against those who might come to desecrate or loot or—

"Jennings!" Steve's shout echoed down the corridor. For a moment, no more than that, Jennings faltered, turned his head. Steve hurried toward him. "Stay where you are!" Confused, Jennings slowed his walk but kept moving. Steve was almost at his side when the floor vanished beneath Jennings' feet. The scientist threw out his arms, his voice a thin cry against the deeper rumble of a huge stone block that moved swiftly into a recess in the *side* of the corridor, leaving in its space a yawning pit. Steve grabbed, his fingers closing on Jennings beneath the man's left arm. He fell to the floor of the corridor, pressing his feet against the stone for leverage. There was nothing to grasp, and he hoped at least the strength of his bionics legs would be great enough to hold him in place. Jennings gasped with pain and shock as Steve held grimly onto him. Mueller and Viejo were beside him at once, grasping Steve's legs, pulling him backward until Wayne got a good grip on Jennings's other arm and hauled him to safety.

They slumped to the floor, Jennings's face white, his chest heaving as he gasped for air. Viejo leaned over the sharp edge where the corridor had been so nakedly exposed. They looked with him. His flashlight played on the bottom of a pit which had jagged spikes stabbing upward. Skeletons were still impaled on the stone spears; bones littered the bottom.

Jennings stared at Steve. "My God, you saved my life."

"Looks that way, doesn't it? And I won't say it was no trouble. Please, Dr. Jennings, take it *easy*..."

They heard Dr. Yavari talking in Spanish to Carla. He was pointing to a stone handle jutting from the wall. It wasn't hard to figure. What Jennings had not seen in his excitement to rush ahead was another bas-relief of symbols and figures. The Caya were not wanton killers. Their rules were clear. One must be able to understand their message, to judge their ciphers, and it was necessary to proceed with the caution and the care that entry into this enormous temple deserved. Yavari translated for them. To proceed with safety beyond this point, what one had to do was to depress an area on the bas-relief. The stone handle would fall into view. If it were pulled down into another recess that opened for it, the stone block would remain safely where it was. Otherwise, the unsuspecting intruder would step on a stone in the corridor that released a drop-weight. Counterbalancing did the rest and the stone was hauled swiftly to the side to suddenly expose the lethal pit. Viejo went to the handle, pulled it down carefully. It completed an arc of one hundred and eighty degrees and a slot appeared in the stone wall to accept the handle. The great stone in the corridor rumbled slowly back into place, settled with a dull booming sound.

Steve looked down the corridor toward the bowl of shifting light. No choice. They had to go that way. They had walked no more than another three or four minutes when they noticed the corridor widening perceptibly. Where it flared to its greatest diameter the dust-swirled light was at its brightest. They moved forward cautiously, the dust under their boots masking the sounds of their shuffling walk. They were like eager yet cautious natives standing in some incomprehensible chamber of an unknown science. They pushed forward until they all were completely within the chamber.

At first it baffled them. Across the wide, circular center floor, a completely open space, they saw the opposite of their corridor. Rudy Wells had been right. Four main corridors traversed the ground level of the temple. All of them arrowed into this hollowed-out center. That they could understand. What they saw, more than these four corridor entrance-ways, left them foundering.

Twelve doorways. Each one sealed. Each doorway crowned with an elaborate bas-relief of *metal*. The first worked metal they had seen, and this was no crude hammering of symbolic jewelry. It had all the appearance of extremely fine etching and engraving in metal. As they brought their lights to bear on the representation over one door, they saw that the metal itself had been worked as if manipulated by . . .

"Good Lord," Jennings said, "it's sculpted . . ."

"Or molded," said Rudy Wells.

"No," Jennings corrected him. "Look, there, it's an individual touch. I'll wager none of these bas-reliefs over the doorways are the same. They're all different. Each is a work of art in itself."

Dr. Yavari moved closer, peering, shaking his head in disbelief. "But . . . is it gold? It does not look like it. It is—"

"An alloy?" Carla prompted.

He looked at her. "They did not have alloys. No metallurgy. This science was not developed." Again he shook his head.

Phil Wayne tapped the metal surface lightly with a fingernail. "I've worked a lot with gold," he said, "and this is *not* gold."

"Then what the hell is it?" They all turned to look at Aaron Mueller, who'd put the question to them.

Wells gave the only answer. "We obviously don't know."

"Should we take a sample back with us?" Mueller was abashed by the stares from Yavari and Jennings.

"No," Yavari said. "Touch nothing! We must study, learn. *Not* damage or desecrate."

Silence followed his words. "I wouldn't recommend removing or taking anything here as a sample," Steve said, in the awkward pause. "We might not survive it." He looked around at the others. "Whoever built this place understood human nature. Maybe it hasn't changed in all the . . . well, in all the years this temple has stood here. Dr. Yavari is probably right. We're better off recording than taking. Phil? Get cracking with those cameras of yours. Aaron and Rudy, give him a hand, will you? Get the lights on those representations for some sharp relief." He turned to Carla. "Can you work with them? Identify whatever you can? And take some notes to go with the pictures. It will help later."

She nodded. "But why are you in such a rush, Steve? These representations"—she gestured—"have been here for thousands of years. They have waited for us all this time. A few hours, or months, or years . . . There is no rush."

"No? Carla, I'm afraid this place is hypnotizing you. You and everybody else." He motioned behind him. "You seem to be forgetting our friends out there. *They'll* be coming in here as soon as they figure out the combination, and I don't intend for us to be in the middle of this shooting gallery to stop them."

"You would leave all *this* to those pirates, Steve? I don't believe you!"

He glanced at Viejo and shook his head, then back to Carla. "Believe me, then. Those people are professionals. They won't mind their manners to get at whatever interests them in this temple."

He turned from her and went to Jennings and Yavari. Carla

looked to Viejo for help. "Unfortunately," Viejo said, "he is right ... unless your words have magic in them, Carla, the kind of magic that can stop explosives and bullets—"

Rudy Wells was talking. "No matter how impossible it seems, there it is. Each doorway apparently represents a period of time roughly corresponding to thirty days. The time isn't so much linked to what we consider our calendar of months, but is close. It seems to have a tie to a worked-out astronomical charting of the heavens. Each doorway, or the representation, the bas-relief, over it would then have a counterpart in one of the signs of the zodiac. I don't mean the astrological equal; at least we can't be sure yet. I'm emphasizing the astronomical, but that could be wrong, too. From here on it's speculation, but at least informed speculation."

In earlier, Air Force days Rudy Wells had earned the wings of a master navigator. As men flew higher and farther and breached the shores of vacuum, he continued his studies in astrogation, the paths along which the astronauts would move. He was also an amateur astronomer of such expertise many considered him a professional in ability. He had combined this background with his love for the ancient peoples of South America and brought this extraordinary knowledge to bear on the mysteries of vanished races which had baffled and confused modern man. At this moment, Rudy Wells was very much in his element. He held a flashlight in one hand, using it as a pointer to sweep the circular chamber. "Three hundred and sixty degrees, give or take a few," he ventured, "although I bet it's dead on. Those symbols? They probably represent a constellation, but I can't figure why they're so much out of line with what we—"

"I've dealt with these same figures," Steve told them. "Celestial navigation. The circle represents the plane of the

168

ecliptic, the path of the sun through a known grouping of stars or groups of stars. The constellations. I think there are two reasons, Rudy, why they seem so strange to you. First, you're forgetting you're in Peru, below the equator. Many of the stars we see here aren't the ones you see in the northern sky. That takes in some constellations, too. That second item I mentioned . . . I recognize some constellations . . . the grouping of stars, not the pictorial representations. As a pilot and an astronaut, well, you know celestial navigation is part of everything we do, or did. If I hadn't lived with the stars so long, I'd hesitate to say this . . . The star charts, or the parts of them they show here, aren't accurate by today's standards. But they surely were accurate when they were prepared."

There was quiet in the chamber. Viejo broke it. "How long ago do you think?"

Steve looked at him. "Ten to twenty thousand years. . . ."

He could have argued the point. Steve wouldn't have budged. One of the serious games the astronauts used to play involved the use of planetarium projectors. In effect they were time machines. They could show the heavens as they would be a thousand or a million years in the future. They could do the same with the past—when Polaris was a long way from being the North Star, for example. Steve found the game fascinating. He would take the time to roll back the ages with the planetarium projector to a thousand and five thousand or more years in the past projected glowingly on the curving walls of the planetarium.

It had come back to him as he studied the representations over the twelve sealed doorways. By his reckoning, the stars and groups of stars they showed in metal were from a time some seventeen thousand years in the past. It was a time long before the first glimmers of civilization, before optics became an experiment, let alone a science, before the mathematics with which to chart the visible heavens had been imagined, and many thousands of years before man invented writing. And yet these many years ago the Caya, if these were the people who built this temple, had mapped the heavens. They had shaped massive stone blocks. And built highways aligned to the cardinal points of the compass. They had used some unknown kind of energy beam to cut and mold their stone monuments. And sculpted metal in alloy form before men even thought of metal. Yet how had they carried or moved these massive stone blocks to this height and built this incredible place?—especially at a time when this enormous temple had looked out across the Sicuani Valley when "men" as the western world knew men were still grubbing in the dirt and painting the walls of their caves—

No more time to think, to speculate. They heard the first muffled explosion far along the corridor that had brought them into this chamber. The sound breached the centuries, brought them jarring into the reality of the moment. No question, at least, about what waited on the other side of that thick stone wall, or that they would be killed if they were caught here.

Where could they go . . . the other three corridors led only to similar exits. Two of them must open to a sheer precipice. The remaining one might be guarded. No time to look for other ways out. Besides, they had only touched the dusty surface of what they had come here to find. To run wasn't the answer; not yet, Steve thought. They had to go *up*. Higher within the temple. Yavari studied a carved inscription by one doorway. He nodded to himself, spoke in Spanish to Carla, who pressed her hand exactly where he told her to apply pressure.

A great stone block moved slowly aside. Jennings flashed his light into the passageway. Steps leading upward, curving out of sight to the left. Quickly the others followed behind Jennings, Viejo taking up the end of the line. When they were

170

all inside, he reached for the stone handle that now extended from the wall within the stairway, pulled it down. The stone rolled back into place.

They climbed the stairs, starting to feel the punishment of dragging their equipment against the steep ascent, sucking in the thin air. One hundred and twenty-eight steps. Exhausted, dizzy, they came to a short corridor. A flashlight beam showed curving walls. Another higher, smaller chamber. Jennings led the way, physically worn but impelled by the adrenalin of his excitement.

They heard a wordless cry from him. Not of fear or shock, but of disbelief. In the chamber, lit by a single beam of sunlight from an aperture in the ceiling, resting on a pedestal in the center of the room, was a toy of exquisite manufacture. They crowded behind Jennings, who saw nothing of the bas-relief in the room, the carved inscriptions. Only that dazzling, beautiful object. He leaned over it, blew away the covering dust.

"It's . . . it's not a toy," he said. "It's . . . incredible."

They saw what he meant. No toy, it was an exquisitely handcrafted model, a scale model, it seemed, of a strange vehicle. Four seats. A control lever of some sort.

No wheels. A tubular arrangement, beneath. It gleamed and sparkled with the tiny jewels used in its making. Jennings moved his hand forward to touch this incredible thing—

Yavari started forward, called out, "Dr. Jennings, *don't* . . . the writing tells—" Jennings didn't hear Yavari. He heard and saw nothing but that presumed key to some wondrous unknown past.

He picked up the jeweled model.

A beam of ghostly blue light stabbed into being. It seemed to come from a tiny hole drilled in stone on the side of the room away from Dr. Jennings.

171

The beam passed through Jennings's heart, winked out. As if it had never been there.

Jennings lay on the floor, a perfectly formed hole starting in his chest that continued through his heart and out his back.

CHAPTER XVII

"I—I WARNED—I shouted to him. I said *wait . . ."* Dr. Yavari turned to his daughter, then to the others. "It is there," he said, pointing at the inscriptions carved into the stone wall behind where Jennings had stood.

"What in God's name does it say?" Rudy Wells demanded.

Carla Yavari answered for her father. "It is a warning that the . . . I don't have the word but it must mean that model or whatever it is that he picked up . . . a warning never to touch or to move it when . . ." Her voice faded.

"When *what?"* Rudy was nearly shouting at her.

"When . . . there is daylight in the sky."

They stared at her. "That's crazy," Mueller said.

"Is it?" Rudy said. "I'll tell you what's crazy." He pointed to the body crumpled on the stone floor. "He's got a perfectly round hole running from his chest to his back. His heart happened to get in the way so it's been drilled, too. Just as if a laser had done the job. Only there are no indications of charring on his clothes and no burns on the skin. Now *that's* what's crazy."

Phil Wayne stooped, examined Jennings, and looked up at Rudy. "He—he didn't know what happened, did he, doc?" There was pain in Wayne's eyes. He had become fond, protective, of the scientist.

"Phil, this man was dead before he could blink his eyes. He never felt a thing," Rudy said. "But I wonder what that thing *was.*"

Wayne straightened. "Well, I can tell you this—I agree it was like a laser beam. You know, the pale light, the coloration. Except I never saw a *blue* laser beam. Red, yellow, white; even a green laser for underwater work. But not blue. It's possible, of course, but any *laser* needs a power source and there isn't any here. It just came out of that damn hole in the wall. What's more, it had a discrete range, it didn't damage anything on the other side of the room. I just checked. And that light, or whatever it was, hit Dr. Jennings the moment he picked up the model . . . there's got to be a triggering device from the pedestal to wherever this thing is directed." He was shaken. "But you people said no one's been in this place for thousands of years. You can't keep something like a laser apparatus on tap for a long period of time . . . And the power . . ."

Steve turned again to Carla. "You said the warning tells whoever's in this room not to pick up that thing while there's daylight—"

"Daylight in the sky, yes."

"Could that mean *sun*light? Not just daylight?"

She glanced at her father and he nodded. "It could, of course. We are not expert at—"

"I understand," Steve said quickly. He glanced upward.

174

"Something connects from this room to whatever's waiting for us upstairs. Some sort of direct line into here."

"That's impossible!" Wayne said, near to shouting in his frustration. "That would mean these people had electricity. *And* an advanced state of electronics . . . and there isn't a sign of that anywhere."

"Right. It's impossible. And Jennings has the neatest hole drilled through him you ever saw. Maybe it isn't electronics, Phil. You could be right."

"Then *what—*"

"We won't find out by standing around here and guessing," Steve said, harsher than he intended. But they all needed a jolt to shake them away from Jennings's death. "Okay, then, we find the way to get upstairs. But we don't need any more lessons in not moving hastily. Agreed?"

Moments later, as they began to pick up their gear, they heard another deep, booming explosion. The sound reached them as a muffled roar, but the signs were unmistakable. Explosives. Big enough to jar the structure itself. Dust shimmered in the air from the vibration.

"Colonel, I think we'd better go down there and check on them," Steve said quickly to Viejo. He bent to his pack, started removing certain items. "The rest of you get moving. If you come to any forked passages, Rudy, leave a marker for us."

He started back down the stairs that had brought them into this chamber, Viejo at his heels. Their flashlights bobbed in crazy flashes as they descended and came to a halt with the huge stone block facing them at the bottom. Viejo pointed to the block. "We must take the chance," he said. Steve knew too well what he meant. He pressed his ear against the stone. Another muffled sound, but he couldn't tell if it came from a distance or was simply muted by the great stone before them. "We've got to open it," he said, and Viejo nodded. "If someone's out there they could start shooting as soon as this thing moves. Well, at least we're in the dark. The moment I hit the level, get flat on that floor. I'll be right with you. If there's trouble, we could just have a slight advantage."

He pressed against the stone by Rudy's marker, instantly dropped flat, his rifle ready. The stone rumbled to the side. No one in the room. Viejo moved out cautiously. Steve closed the stone behind them; no use leaving a sign pointing to where the others had gone. Another blast, much louder now, spun them around. "The corridor," Viejo said. "They're trying to blow the entrance open."

"Which means they don't know how to work those pressure points." Dust rolled toward them from the corridor they had taken when they first entered the temple. "Well, that shows they've broken through," Steve said. "They'll be coming in here soon."

"We will welcome them," Viejo said.

"Let's do that," Steve agreed. Viejo was a bantam rooster, spoiling for a fight even now.

Steve reached around for his pack and the surprises he had brought along. Their best tack was to convince Fossengen's men that coming into the temple along any of the corridors was the same as suicide. That meant hitting them hard and confusing the survivors. And then, if they could surprise them . . .

Another thundering blast, and they saw a flash of daylight at the far outside end of the corridor. Steve and Viejo went prone, each to a side of the corridor, their rifles on automatic and pointing into the corridor. When it was time, no need even to aim. Another wave of choking dust boiled from the corridor into the big chamber. They waited, muffling coughs with their hands. Footsteps. Two or three of them, by the sound of it. They still waited, until Viejo motioned for Steve's attention, pointing. A bobbing light; a flash held in a man's hand as he walked. They heard low voices. They still waited, until the first forms were visible. Viejo looked at Steve and he nodded. They opened fire.

Short bursts, hammering bullets into the corridor under high velocity. Screams, the continued shattering roar of the rifles. The corridor became a wasp's nest filled with whining lead creatures, ricocheting off the corridor walls, continuing the length of the long passage, tearing and chopping into anything that came within reach. Their clips were empty. They slammed in fresh clips. Steve reached into a pocket, pulled out a smoke grenade. He jerked the pin and threw the grenade as hard as he could into the tunnel. Before it hit the floor, thick, acrid, orange smoke billowed out. "That'll slow anybody," Steve said.

They moved swiftly. They'd come into the temple from its southwest corner. There was the chance they could provide another surprise to the opposition, make them think Steve's people had left some covering firepower outside. They ran steadily along the corridor leading to the northwest corner of the temple. At the end, as Viejo gasped for air, Steve flashed his light on a bas-relief he expected to find by the stone. It was there. "Wait"—he looked to Viejo—"the tunnel ... we have been running, yet there have been no deadfalls."

Steve also had forgotten completely ... but then he realized the traps would be set for someone coming *into* the tunnel, not leaving. Still, Viejo was absolutely right, they'd better keep it in mind on the way back. But what about those men who'd come along that first corridor? Well, it was obvious they hadn't reached its deadfall yet. Maybe their next group would ...

He pressed against the stone. The huge block moved aside slowly, creaking. He placed his hand against the exposed side, pushed as hard as he could. The stone moved halfway, stopped, jammed, but they had enough room to get through.

They moved outside, crouching, facing a growth of tall grass and vines. Good cover. "Colonel, stay under cover here and keep an eye on me. I just might need some help."

Before Viejo could protest, Steve was gone, staying close to the huge temple flank. He reached a low hill on which great stones and boulders had tumbled. The cover he needed. Crouching, he broke to his right to reach heavy undergrowth. He moved closer to where they had first approached the temple.

He froze. Ten? Fossengen had more than twenty men with him, a group milling around the corridor entrance. Steve saw the opening. They *had* blasted their way in. He studied the cover about him. He set the rifle carefully and squeezed off five quick shots. Two men spun about and fell. The rifle reports were still echoing off the temple when he ducked low and ran with all the speed he could manage in the undergrowth *away* from where Viejo waited. He threw himself prone, saw the others, under cover now, firing into the growth from where he had just fired. He aimed carefully, squeezed off three rounds, saw another man tumble to the ground. Again his speed was his only defense, and he was back into the growth. He stopped once, fired a long burst at the group, kept on going. If the reaction was as he hoped, then Fossengen had to figure on a pretty substantial force of unknown size to his rear. He couldn't leave himself without cover in that direction, and that would cut his forces even more. Steve kept on running, reached the hill with its haphazardly strewn boulders, and broke back toward the base of the temple. Shots cracked from behind him and buzzed by his ears. Another bullet spanged off rock just over his head. He kept running. Almost there. Viejo came into view, on one knee, firing single rounds one after the other, covering him.

They tumbled through the narrow opening back into the corridor. Steve's chest heaved as he fought to breathe. He didn't try to talk, gesturing instead at the door control. Viejo got to his feet, pressed. The stone rumbled part way, then stopped. Bullets slammed into the stone from the other side. Steve and Viejo glanced at each other, then at the stone block. At its base was a spent cartridge, jamming the bottom of the groove along which the stone moved. Viejo banged his hand against the release and the stone opened. Quickly he slammed the door control again, then stooped to brush aside the empty cartridge. The doorway was half closed when a burst caught Viejo in the neck and chest, hurling him back into the corridor. He tumbled twice, came to rest in a heap, half his neck shot away.

Steve was hardly aware that the stone block had slid back into its resting place, sealing off the corridor from the outside. For a long moment he stared at the man who had become his friend. He removed the cartridge belt from Viejo's body. He turned and started back along the corridor, running steadily. Barely in time he remembered, slowed his speed, used his flashlight to search for the bas-relief on the wall. He found it, pressed, watched the handle emerge. He pulled it down and felt it lock in place. It was now safe to continue.

He found the central chamber still empty. Orange smoke hung in the air. That same draft from unknown places stirred it slowly. Steve crossed the chamber, worked the door control to the stairway that led to the group waiting for him in the room high in the temple.

He told them how Viejo had died. And the rest of it, including the size of the force Fossengen had brought with him. "It's getting late," he finished, "we've got to get set for the night . . . higher than we are now. There's still a lot of temple above us."

Rudy Wells pointed to one of the panels. "Right there," he told Steve. "We found it while you were gone."

179

"Where does it lead to?"

"We didn't go up. Figured it was best that we wait for you. Dr. Yavari thinks it's the main room of the temple. The high point. Probably some way of looking out over the local countryside from there."

Steve nodded. "We can use that. All right, everybody be ready to move out of here."

At least the Caya followed the principle of repetition. Each doorway worked as the others. The expected stone block slid aside, and their flashlights showed a curving stairway of stone. But the width was less than the others, and the curvature tighter.

Exactly half as many steps as the first stairway. Sixty-four smoothly cut ledges of stone fitted together perfectly. Steve stayed in the lead, his rifle held loosely. He figured it wouldn't be of any use against whatever the Caya might have left behind. He walked slowly, carefully, the searching light in his hand prodding the way for him. He stopped and looked back to Mueller. "I see it," Mueller said. "Another chamber, it looks like from here."

Steve nodded. "Maybe *the* chamber."

They moved slowly from the stairs just as the sun was slipping beneath distant peaks. The deep red wash of sunset etched its way through the jagged gorges, stabbed at the great western flanks of the temple. But up here, as Yavari had anticipated, there was light.

Steve looked at the thin line of sunlight showing through one wall. He turned the flash on it, saw a stone fitted perfectly for a window space shoved partially into the chamber. So that was how they worked it. They had no glass and yet they needed protection from the elements up here. High winds, torrential rains. Over each slot, carved, *burned* through the stone with a convergence, another stone was suspended, to be moved into its matching slot like a heavy plug when desired.

With all the slots so fitted, or plugged, the high chamber was sealed off from the world. Whatever had been used to suspend the window stones had been gone for thousands of years. Rotted away. Only the stones remained, all of them in their slots. Except the one dislodged by wind, or tremor, or lightning bolt. It didn't matter. Steve leaned his rifle against the wall, lifted the stone free, brought it gently to the floor. The last touch of sunset poured into the room.

Aaron Mueller gasped, a sharp intake of breath, and Steve turned around, ready for whatever—

He froze. In the center of the room, concealed within shadows until the stone was removed from the window slot, now catching and reflecting the last rays of the sun, above their heads, impossible, magnificent, iridescent from a thousand twists of light within its substance.

The high crystal.

CHAPTER XVIII

EIGHT FEET high. Five feet across at its widest point. Multi-faceted. Impossible. In the chamber, the window slot closed off so no light from their battery lamps would show, they stared and spoke in quiet tones to one another. It was hypnotic. Centuries gave off their own aura. It overpowered them with its presence and what it meant in terms of time and a vanished race. It answered questions, gave basis to a thousand rumors, posed ten thousand questions more. It pushed their physical trials from their minds, banished the deaths of Jennings and Viejo to another plane of thought.

The questions poured at them. "Notice the sloping sides of the thing?" Rudy said, pointing with his flashlight. "No dust . . ."

Heads turned to Phil Wayne. "The only reasonable

answer," he said slowly, "is that the crystal has some electric field property. Electrostatic ... whatever it is it rejects anything, including dust settling on it."

"Hey, over here!" They joined Aaron Mueller studying a neatly drilled hole, round, extending into the floor. There were eleven others, equally spaced about the room. "Now we know how Jennings was killed," Mueller said. "That cavity you see there must extend into the chamber where Jennings picked up the model."

"It doesn't make sense," Carla protested. "The light that killed him was horizontal. This is perhaps seventy or eighty degrees."

Wayne came closer. "No, he's right. In that chamber below us there's either an optical reflector system or another, much smaller crystal. You could bend that kind of beam thirty or eighty degrees without any problem."

"Optics?" Rudy Wells said. "That means grinding, lenses, understanding the optical properties. They didn't *have* optics."

"Right, doc. You show me there isn't any crystal in this room either, and I'll sure agree with you," Wayne said. "It also means that each chamber has this same kind of booby trap built into it. Maybe worse."

"Don't blame *them,*" Carla said. "They protected what they left behind. That's all. *And* gave every one of us a clear warning. Dr. Jennings couldn't wait. If only he had waited just another few seconds . . ."

Steve forced himself to sound harsh, and worried he'd overdone it. "Tomorrow is what concerns me now, and it should concern all of you. Viejo's dead too, and that *wasn't* accidental." He looked up, studying the curving upper walls of the dome. "Phil, you've got work to do. We need every one of those diagrams in the stone photographed. Don't leave out anything." The stone panels were perhaps even more important than the crystal, for they broke down the crystal design from all sides, showed how it received sunlight, how it could be beamed. "You've got two cameras," Steve went on. "Shoot one series in color and one in black-and-white." Wayne nodded. "When you're finished, seal the color in a watertight bag and give it to me. You keep the black-and-white the same way. Rudy, stay with Phil. Use that tape recorder. Make any notes you think are pertinent. Start over there. Mark it panel number one and go clockwise around the dome. The sooner we get this on film and tape the better." He looked at them all. "We may have to execute that well known maneuver of getting the hell out of here, and soon. Fossengen and his crew are likely to get impatient."

Mueller spoke up. "They could just try to starve us out, Steve."

"Sure, but I doubt it. They can't wait us out too long. They want what we've found. This temple, these massive stone blocks, this construction . . . its message of a power beyond anything we know today about controlled energy. . . . Something that could change the face of our whole civilization. No, I don't think they'll sit and wait for us to give up. Those people out there," Steve said slowly, "are going to do whatever they feel necessary to get their hands on this"—he indicated the crystal—"or to keep us from getting back to our respective governments with this information. If they can't get it, they'll try to destroy it. And us."

The huge crystal was balanced on a series of thin, metal-like rods in the form of push-pull arms so that it might be tilted at different angles. It was the only place they had seen metal in the temple except for some of the bas-relief plates. The push-pull arms were set in a circle of stone so that the entire device could be rotated about its axis, like a stone ring within a groove. It appeared it would move with no more energy

185

required than could be delivered by one man. Steve elected not to try that movement yet, until he better understood this incredible apparatus. In the "front" of the crystal, directly below its centerline, he saw a circular indentation about eleven inches in diameter. It was obviously a lens within the much greater "lens capacity" of the crystal itself. Now that he had this clearly in his mind, Steve searched for and discovered smaller circular lenses on each side of the crystal—he counted four in all; the main lens, and the smaller ones, no more than an inch in diameter. He felt sure that whatever energy was fed into the crystal could be channeled through any one of the four lenses. He had worked with all kinds of complicated, exquisite equipment. He had solid background for this judgment.

The arrangement of the crystal facets, the main lens and three smaller lenses, and the push-pull arms suggested that by moving the arms, and rotating the crystal on its ring, you could effectively aim or direct the energy that had to come from the lens—in this case the largest circle. None of them had any idea what the material was that made up the crystal. They only had suggestions, supported by hard knowledge. Not even Phil Wayne who had lived and worked with crystals as a mechanic, as a mechanic would work with tools and an engine, would hazard a guess.

The energy, they were convinced, was solar. Yavari translated the strange glyphs on the walls. The ancient schematics and diagrams, which was what they turned out to be, indicated only solar light as the source of energy for the crystal. If there had been some other energy involved, then it was no longer here. There'd be argument on that point later on when engineers got their hands on this extraordinary package, because the temple could never have been assembled by manpower alone. Other energies had been used here. Right now, though, the crystal was everything.

The slots cut so neatly into the outer walls of the temple dome . . . At a certain time of day the sun would strike directly in a beam channeled through a slot to the crystal. There, something inexplicable happened to that gentle beam of sunlight. Its intensity was somehow magnified thousands of millions of times within the matrix of the crystal, and what emerged through the aiming lens had to be an energy beam of unspeakable violence. Steve wondered about the "lightning" that had assaulted Major Ryland's plane . . .

Carla discovered the dome itself could be moved. It would slide back, Steve reckoned, so that at high noon, with the sun at its fiercest, the solar energy would fall full onto the crystal from directly overhead. That would be the most intense of all energy levels, and what the beam would or could do under that power was staggering to contemplate. Wayne had talked of a super laser beam, as far advanced over what they did with rubies and crystals in their lasers as a laser was advanced over an ordinary flashlight beam. If this were so, then the Caya—or whoever had taught the Caya—knew how to utilize the energy in a solar beam so they could control coherent light without the necessary pumping systems of lasers.

If the Caya could build or could get their hands on a crystal of this size there was every chance they worked with crystals of smaller dimension and/or lesser energy. And that would explain the manner in which these stones had been cut so perfectly, how one stone went atop the other so smoothly they seemed to have been extruded. It was super-laser welding of a sort that would handle stone or metal or any substance one might imagine. And, Steve reflected, if you could control this sort of energy down to an *nth* level, then you could transmit energy. Like a microwave system, but so advanced the microwave pulse system would seem like a tugboat whistle.

And that would help explain something of the strange jeweled model in that lower chamber . . . why bother with wheels if you could have power transmission of *that* level? The model had a kind of antenna, or receiving dish, and if this picked up beamed energy, it could translate that energy into a repulsion system. (Could there be something buried beneath that glazed surface of the highway?) The principle wasn't so extraordinary. Magnetic repulsors had been tested for years for superfast trains. And beaming energy, even massive bolts of plasma with the fury of a nuclear fireball, was the kind of program into which the United States and the Soviet Union, in their competitive efforts to develop a system for knocking out the warheads of incoming missiles, had been pouring billions of dollars for years.

So this crystal could be ... Steve felt the chill move slowly through him. In this most ancient room could be the quantum jump into the future of energy control. It could revolutionize industry. It could make enormous levels of power available to the smallest hamlet anywhere in the world. The energy crisis would be a near-overnight bad memory only. It represented a colossal economic force. It was—

A weapon. Unlike any other. Coupled with the latest laser systems for pumping vast energy pulses through ... Steve shook his head. A quantum jump in destructive power. That also was in this room.

And outside, a group of men who needed to kill them to grasp this reach into the future of unparalleled energy control. He looked at the crystal and knew it was another extension of that moment when the atom climbed from mystery into men's daily affairs.

If possible, he would bring the secret of the crystal home. In any event, he would do whatever he could to prevent the secret from falling into the hands of the people Fossengen worked for. He had to smile to himself. Steve Austin, military adventurer. When they'd gone to the moon to explore the distant past they hadn't needed so much as a popgun. Weapons were hardly relevant against the far more dangerous adversary of cold and the weightless state in space where gravity didn't exist, where—

Gravity. *Where it didn't exist.* It came to him with a shock that perhaps this was behind the secret of the crystal, of the special energy that literally had moved mountains. The crystal ... what, indeed, if it *didn't* originate with the Caya? What if there was some truth to the old legends ... the Chariots of the Gods ... *What if the crystal had been brought here* ... Perhaps, then, the crystal from gravityless space was somehow linked to an anti-grav force ...

Anti-gravity ... It was a matter of degree. An airplane was an anti-gravity machine of sorts. So was the Saturn V that had boosted a hundred thousand pounds to the moon on Steve's own mission. But these were basically inefficient. They *fought* gravity; they didn't eliminate it. This crystal was obviously a means of power transmission. Not a new idea. Scientists had been experimenting with microwave transmission for a long time, without much luck. These ancients were far advanced over them with their power systems and lasers. But what if the crystal was also a *means* of transmitting enormous quantities of energy? He visualized a huge ship receiving an energy beam transmitted through the crystal, the energy channeled into repulsors.

That wouldn't be crude *anti*-gravity. It would be null-g, null-gravity! A smooth, complete blanking out of gravitational force. The nudge of a finger, so to speak, would be enough to ease a ship away from a planet. Or raise a heavy stone to great heights. The possibilities were nearly beyond belief. If there was substance to his notion, then the crystal could potentially open up the entire solar system to men's exploration. ...

189

A fine dream, but now the reality was more urgent. He looked about him. Wayne and Rudy were wrapping up their photography and taping work. Fatigue was closing the eyes of Dr. Yavari, and his daughter was arranging a makeshift bed from their packs. Mueller was in the stairwell, listening for any sign of movement. It was going to be a long night. In the morning, Steve decided, they would test the crystal.

CHAPTER XIX

"DR. YAVARI and Carla have been plotting the sun angles. I've looked at it from a different point of view, but we check out," Rudy Wells said, tapping a sketch of the dome. "At just about ten o'clock this morning, a few minutes from now, slot number three, that's over there, will drop a shaft of sunlight directly into the crystal. We'll have to work those push-pull gimmicks to bring the crystal down a bit. Now directly in front of the main lens—you can see the outline on the wall—there's about a four-foot section of stone. The way Dr. Yavari reads the inscription, the whole section slides to the side. The crystal beams through there."

Steve studied the sketches. It seemed to fit as Rudy explained it. He told Mueller to take up his position in the stairwell again. Once they started working with this thing they'd be wrapped up so tight in it they wouldn't hear an elephant tripping over his own legs.

He wondered about Fossengen. Nothing had been heard the night through. They'd taken turns at guard, but outside of animal and bird sounds, and the constant wind, they seemed to be in a deserted world.

"Stay back from the open spaces when we move the stones," he warned the others. "Fossengen and his people will be watching for anything. We may be high up but we're a target for a sniper with a scope." He looked around. "Everyone ready? Okay, Rudy, the stone."

The doctor went to the western side of the dome, pressed against a circular space in the carved inscription. Something scraped and complained with a loud squealing sound, and then the four-foot block of stone slid along a groove to the right.

"Back from there," Steve snapped at Rudy, who stepped away from the yawning space in the dome wall. Light flooded the room, bringing new life to the crystal. It glowed from a thousand different places and, as they studied it, searched within the bottomless twisting of light, the points of reflection and glow shifted and took up fractions of an inch away. It seemed to warp vision. Dust blew about them, the wind leaping through the open space, blowing away time and indecision. This was what it was like *then,* to the Caya priests and their men of knowledge. This was how *they* felt perhaps seventeen thousand years ago . . .

"Phil, the stone behind you. Number three slot. When you remove it, put it on the floor and then come here next to me. I want you to be the one to lower the crystal."

Wayne nodded. He worked the shaped stone free from the wall slot, brought it to the floor. A beam of sunlight stood frozen, almost material, in the dust swirling about them. But it

192

did not reach the crystal. Not yet, for it was still high over its mount on the push-pull arms.

Wayne joined Steve, grasped the control rods, really no more than simple levers. He turned to Steve, waiting.

"It's time," Steve said.

Wayne moved the levers. The crystal came down slowly and steadily. Wayne felt a slight click, and the crystal was in place. The sunlight from the open slot flowed into and was lost within the crystal.

Light shifted before their eyes. They still looked at the crystal, couldn't focus. Light shimmered and danced before them. A vibration filled the room. It could almost be heard but it wasn't sonic. Something disturbed the air.

It happened.

A beam of light, pale blue, white also, snapped into existence. A single unbelievably intense flash, real and unreal, impossible and overwhelming in its reality, just ... *existed.* The ghostly radiance flashed away, visible for thousands of feet, and flickered out of sight.

"Phil, lift it up!" Steve directed. Wayne moved the control levers, raised the crystal from its resting place.

Steve studied his watch. "Four seconds. The beam was there for just four seconds, and then it vanished. Why?"

Wayne was still shaken, but he took hold of himself. "The pulse," he said. "Whatever happens inside that crystal, it seems to rearrange light. From random to coherent, like a laser. But ... I don't know what happens in there, Steve, only that it works. You saw it. We all did. The crystal does something with direct solar radiation. God knows what. When it, well, when it builds up what we call a charge, it pulses it out. Four seconds. Then the charge is gone. It starts all over again."

"How long between pulses?"

"Your guess is as good as mine."

193

"Let's find out. That last one just went out into thin air. Did you notice anything special about it?"

"Sure," Wayne said at once. "Ionization effect in the air. Also some electrostatic fielding. Did you hear that slight rumble?"

Steve wasn't sure and said so. "Well, on a small scale, you were hearing thunder. The beam burns through the air. You've got heating and expansion. Shock wave."

"And I thought you weren't paying attention," Steve said. "Look, that hill over there," he said, pointing. "How far?"

"Thousand yards, maybe a little less," Wayne replied.

"Think the beam can reach it?"

"It went three times that distance, Steve. I'm sure there's a range control somewhere, but I haven't—"

"Later for that. Okay, Phil. Before you bring it down again, can you aim at the top of that hill?"

He did, angling the position of the large center lens. Then he lowered the crystal again. They waited. It took ten seconds before the ghostly blue beam flicked into existence.

A thousand yards away the summit of the hill *boiled.* No other word for it. Flame speared upward as the beam slashed through trees, earth and rocks. The foliage burst into flame. The heat had to go somewhere. Within a second, faster than their eyes could follow what was happening, rocks ran molten, spattering blazing globules in all directions. A screaming sound drifted toward them.

The beam snapped out.

They were stunned. They stared at the tight circle of carnage in the distance. Smoke spumed before the wind.

"Rudy, relieve Mueller on the stairs. I want our State Department to see what kind of tiger we've got by the tail."

Mueller came into the domed chamber. Steve pointed. "When Phil brings the crystal into position, we get a pale blue beam," he said. "And that's what happens." Mueller looked at the blackened earth, the flames barely seen on the slope, the smoke pouring before the wind. "I want you to see it for yourself," Steve continued. Then, to Wayne: "Phil, when you bring it down this time, as soon as we get the beam, move it slightly from left to right. A sawing motion. Okay, let's have it again."

Wayne brought the crystal down, waited. Ten seconds.

Snap.

The ghostly radiance leaped into being. From the crystal to the far hill, instantly.

Wayne moved it from side to side.

The top of the hill exploded.

Not a blast. A continuing, ripping explosion occurring everywhere the beam touched. The crystal trembled beneath Wayne's own shaking hands. The tremble was magnified by distance to a slight up-and down motion along with the sawing effect. The side of the hill was torn to pieces. Flames everywhere. Cracking blasts, overlaid by a shattering roar.

Snap.

The beam was gone. The top of the hill was gone. Below, molten rock tumbled and splashed. The line of trees and brush blazed. Wayne raised the crystal.

Mueller stared. He went to the open space, his hands resting on the stone, still staring.

"Aaron! Get back from that—"

Steve didn't finish the warning. Mueller turned from the open space, one hand raised, his mouth open. He tried to speak but the blood spilled from his mouth and down over his clothes. A black hole showed in his chest, immediately below the neck. He collapsed to the floor.

"Down! Everybody down!"

The sniper's second bullet ricocheted off stone. Rudy

195

scrabbled forward on the floor, reached up to bang his hand against the control. Stone rumbled back into place. Wayne slammed the other form-fitting stone into the window slot.

Someone groped for a flashlight. When it came on they heard her cry out. Carla.

"Oh, my God," Rudy said, rushing to her side. The second bullet, ricocheting off the wall, had struck Dr. Yavari in the head. Fatally.

CHAPTER XX

PHIL WAYNE said it calmly, almost like casual conversation, as he attended to his cameras. "We're trapped."

Steve nodded, sat on the floor of the domed chamber, his back against a wall, resting his forearms on his knees. Carla still suffered from shock, but she'd refused any sedatives from Rudy Wells. A good sign. The girl was strong. She would rally. She would have to.

They all would, Steve thought. When they'd come to this temple there had been eight of them. Now they were half that number. In cold-blooded terms of survival chances, losing Mueller, and especially Viejo, was particularly serious. The Peruvian officer was more than a fighter; he was native to this vicious high jungle country.

Well, at least we know the rules now, Steve thought.

Anything goes. Which could work both ways. He wondered if he wasn't pumping himself full of bravado. They were penned like rats in this tower. Certainly Fossengen had figured out the four main entrances to the temple, and waiting outside each would be one or more men with automatic weapons zeroed in on the doorways.

Think, he told himself. He considered and instantly dismissed the possibility of making some sort of deal with Fossengen. Fossengen couldn't afford to leave a single one of them alive. Well, the lines were drawn. Find a way out of here, or join the ancient dust of this place.

It had to be soon. Fossengen's men would start scaling the walls. There were enough breaks in the surface, along with vines and other growth that had had thousands of years to get purchase in stone, for a good man to work his way to the top and then set up lines for others to follow. After that it would be only a matter of time before explosive charges did the rest.

Steve looked at the crystal. He'd made up his mind what to do about the incredible device, as well as the schematics and panels engraved in stone and metal. The slow view he took of the dome charged his thinking. The old priests, the men who once ran this temple and conducted the affairs of the local tribes, they'd had more problems than bands of natives. They doubtless had their power plays among the hierarchy—Steve guessed the Caya weren't so far ahead of the rest of the human race to have avoided old-fashioned, human in-fighting.

He sat up straight. That meant those who once were in charge of this temple must have provided a way out in emergencies. A back door open—which would have been easy enough to manage for those in charge of building the place, and who kept the secret by killing off the work crew after the job was completed.

Steve called the others, laid out for them exactly what his thoughts had been and the conclusion he'd reached. They turned on every light they had and began scouring the dome.

It took Carla two hours to find it. In all the dome there was one bas-relief that didn't fit. It served no apparent purpose, which was its secret. The carvings they'd found had been functional, not ornamental. Carla sat on the floor by the west side of the dome, a face-mask carving under bright lights, and studied its every detail. She leaned forward slowly, running her fingers along the stone. She hesitated, applied pressure. Nothing. Carla studied the bas-relief even more carefully. Again she applied pressure, and again nothing. She sat back and Rudy Wells joined her.

"It could be you're right about that relief being the key," Rudy speculated, "but maybe you're going about it the wrong way. I don't know, but if you were one of the old temple leaders, why use the same system for getting in and out of this place, through the regular corridors, that you'd use for your emergency exit. They would—"

Carla didn't let him finish. "Of course!" She turned again to the carving, placed her hands so that she was applying pressure to each side of the figures. Again, nothing. She looked at them in despair.

"It's been thousands of years," Steve said. "Let me try. Is this where the pressure goes?" She nodded, and he brought his bionics hand to the bas-relief, pressed in, twisted. The ornamental carving turned with the pressure of those powerful fingers. Groaning sounds came from within a nearby wall. "You were right all the time," Steve told her. "But it's been so long since this has moved—dust, humidity, maybe even some insects jammed it."

"It's not jammed any more. That's for sure," Phil Wayne said. "Look!" In the northwest corner of the room they stared at black space where there had been a heavy stone. Two feet wide by four feet high. Just right to accommodate a man.

Wayne leaned through the space with a flashlight. When he

straightened his body and turned around, the smile on his face was gone.

"What's wrong?" Carla asked.

"It's a shaft."

"That's all we need," Rudy told him. "The best thing we could have—"

"It's a shaft with four walls straight down. A couple of hundred feet, I think. And nothing to hold on to."

Steve went to the shaft, probed it with his flashlight. The light shone from the walls of the shaft, but he could see nothing straight down. Impossible, really, to tell just how far it went before it hit bottom. Rudy brought him a thin plastic-lined cable from their equipment pack. Moments later the cable was lowering one of their strong lights down the shaft. It hit bottom on what looked to be stone. Staring downward, the light seemed almost to smoke or twist in their vision. Wayne started hauling up the flashlight, measuring off the depth of the shaft with the cable.

"Well, we know a few good things," Rudy said. "The shaft is clear all the way down. No obstructions. It seems to be dry down there, which is important. And we didn't see any snakes."

"Which doesn't mean they are not there," Carla quickly warned.

Rudy nodded, turned to watch Wayne. "How far down?" he asked.

Wayne whistled, and not with pleasure. "About two hundred and thirty feet. *That* is tough."

"Not as bad as it could be," Steve said.

"You kidding? Two hundred and thirty feet not bad? That's like trying to climb down a rope from the top floor of a building that's twenty-three stories high!"

Steve didn't answer as he leaned into the deep shaft to look not down but up. Sure enough, about four feet above the space through which he leaned were three loops of metal, like eyebolts, through which a safety line or rope could be passed. He took a tripod from Wayne's camera equipment, tapped one of the metal loops. As quickly as the end of the tripod brushed against the metal loop, it fell apart in rusted fragments and dust.

Steve came out of the shaft brushing dust and particles from his face, and told the others what had happened. "Still," he said, "we've got a thousand feet of cable and—"

"What strength?" Wayne asked.

"Three thousand pound test."

They looped the cable twice around the great stand in the center of the dome. Without eyebolts or similar equipment they had little control over hanging the cable dead-center in the shaft, and trying to work down the cable promised to be almost impossible.

"How are we going to manage this thing?" Wayne said in exasperation. "Steve, that plastic around the cable is slick. I'm pretty strong but I'd never be able to lower myself all that distance without slipping. When your hands start to sweat . . . anyway, it'd be suicide. And what happens if we cut off the plastic? The cable is thin. Right through your skin, or it would at least start to burn you if you went too fast. I don't know . . ."

Steve and Rudy glanced at one another, said nothing about a bionics hand with its extraordinary gripping strength.

"I'll go down first," Steve said. "Check it out. See if there's a way out through the bottom." A dull boom echoed through the structure. Dust spilled gently from the ceiling. "And I don't think we have very much more time to discuss it. Rudy, what Phil just said about that cable was right. Tape me up good." He extended his right hand. Quickly Rudy padded the palm with heavy gauze, then wrapped the hand in adhesive tape, leaving the fingers enough flexibility to be bent. Steve donned the gunbelt with the revolver, loaded gear into his pockets and went to the shaft entrance. He tested his grip on the cable. He turned to the others. "Phil, take the pack webbing from the bodies"—he nodded to the canvas-covered forms on the floor. "Wire two of them together and make a body sling like a parachute harness. That's how the rest of you are getting out of here."

He slipped into the shaft. Rudy leaned into the shaft above him, playing a flashlight beam toward the bottom. Steve ran the cable between his boots, using friction to control his descent. Actually his movement down the cable that so worried Wayne was relatively easy. His legs weren't even strained by the effort, and by gripping the cable in his bionics left hand he had no problem about perspiration or skin burns. The tape on his right hand was a just-in-case precaution, and at the same time was a show of normal precaution for the others who, otherwise, would have wondered and asked questions.

He went down slowly, looking at the four walls of the shaft. The dryness surprised him. No evidence of major leakage or water flow. Of course insects had gotten in, and he dropped slowly through ancient spiderwebs. But even the spiders must have found the insect population too low to bother with, and nothing was seen moving during the long and careful descent. Then he was down, the flashlight showing small crushed stones for underfooting. He kept his left hand on the cable, applied pressure slowly. Firm, but not completely dry. That, too, he expected. He was in some form of cave. He moved the flashlight slowly, stopped, frozen in position. Reflections. *Eyes.* He moved the light. Rats. Huge. The rodents watched unafraid. No reason for them to be scared of anything, thought Steve. They've got no enemies down here except maybe snakes. There was at least a fifty-fifty chance the rats wouldn't bother him.

Heavy undergrowth. Mostly vines. He removed a thick candle from a pocket, placed it on the ground, and lit it. The flame speared up momentarily, sending lights dancing on the low cave walls. Then it settled down. Steve waited. The flame moved. Bent over to the right. Kept flickering in that direction. So the way out had to be to the left. He moved the candle closer to the growth, brought the flashlight to bear. A tangled matting. He went back to the shaft, told Wayne to send down the machete.

About an hour later he had hacked his way through, and daylight showed through an opening not quite two feet off the ground. Outside the temple there was more growth that hid the opening. He blew out the candle and snapped off the flashlight, working his way carefully to the opening. A ledge extended several feet from the temple wall, then fell away in a steep drop. Steve grabbed some of the brush he'd cut loose, held a thick swatch over himself, and inched his way to the end of the ledge.

The steep slope ended about three or four hundred feet down. A heavy copse of trees showed how solid it was. He looked left and right. Sheer drops from the temple wall. Unlikely that anyone would think of looking for somebody along this flank. No hint of an exit showed. Still, during daylight there was always the chance of being spotted. Animals or birds could set up a racket at any disturbance. The time to go was at night. This same night, in a few hours. They'd need all the lead they could get.

He retraced his steps back into the low cave. He left the candle and the machete behind. Wayne called down from the chamber. "We'll pull you up. Hang on."

"No, just make sure the cable is secured to that pedestal." Wayne's face disappeared to be replaced by Rudy Wells's. He heard an exchange of words, then Rudy signaled him to start up. He held position with his right arm, the cable twined between his boots. He reached up with his left arm and hauled, then repeated the same move. He made it up the 230 feet. He glanced at Rudy and slipped back into the chamber, just in time to feel another heavy blast elsewhere in the temple.

"We're down to no margin," he said, told what he'd discovered at the bottom of the shaft and outlined his plan. "We strip ourselves of everything except what we need to exist for a few days, and I mean *everything*. We go as light as we can. We take food, some water, medical supplies and weapons, and that's it. Only exception is the film. I've got one set and Phil has the other."

"What about my camera gear?" Wayne asked.

"Forget it. We get home, I promise Uncle Sam will buy you anything you want."

Wayne looked unhappily at his equipment.

"How about that harness?" Steve asked.

Rudy held it up. "It's here and it works. We tried it out."

"Okay. Get your packs ready the way I told you. We've got three or four hours of daylight left and I want to be moving the moment it gets dark. Rudy, you'll go down first. Carla next. Then Phil and I have a few things to attend to in here. We'll follow right behind."

He saw Carla looking at her father's body. "I'm sorry, Carla. There's nothing we can do."

She nodded, holding back tears.

An hour before darkness Steve lowered Rudy down the shaft. He brought up the cable with the harness, fastened it around Carla, and she was sent down. Then their packs, all prepared to be put on the moment they were ready. Steve turned to Wayne. "No one's going to like us for what happens next," he said. Wayne waited. "We're going to leave a booby trap."

"In *here?* Steve, the crystal . . ."

"You know its potential, don't you?"

204

"Well, I guess so ... after all, I work in this field, remember?"

"How'd you like it to end up in the wrong hands?"

"It's not that simple, Steve. I mean, you think of something like that crystal, and what good it can do ... I don't know. I really—don't—*know.*"

Steve looked at the crystal. "Maybe I can make the choice easier for you. No political speeches. Just a question. What do you think would happen in the world today if a hostile, aggressive nation were the only one to have the hydrogen bomb?"

"I get your drift."

"We don't *know,*" Steve said, "but I wouldn't like to test it."

"No, I guess not. All right, Steve, what do we do?"

"In my pack. Primer cord. I've also got six packets of plastic explosive left. We rig this room. Tape a detonator wire to the entrance down below. A trip wire up here as a back-up. A pressure pad we can rig for the floor as a third safety. Three shots at it. If anyone gets into this room any way except back up this shaft"—he pointed to their escape route—"the whole place goes. Not just the crystal. There's enough stuff here to take out this entire chamber. If Fossengen and his people don't get in here, no harm done. If they do—"

Wayne sighed. "Let's get started."

They finished about thirty minutes later. "We've got to let Fossengen think we're holed up here for the night," Steve said. "When I come through the shaft behind you, I'll close the passage. There's a control inside the shaft for the stone that'll put it back into place. Just before we do that, I'll remove one of the window stones. I'll leave a light on the floor. They'll see it. They might spend the night taking shots at us every now and then, to keep us away from the window. Anyway, it'll help keep them busy."

He sent Wayne down the shaft. They'd cut three hundred

feet from the cable for the job of getting down the shaft. They would need the remainder for dropping down the side of the cliff.

Steve placed a battery lamp on the floor, turned on the switch. He removed one of the window stones, went quickly to the shaft. He was inside the shaft, grasping the cable and preparing to return the heavy stone to its place when he heard the distant report of an automatic rifle. Bullets ripped into the window, several of them making their way into the chamber. Just before the stone slid back into place he saw a crack start in the crystal, spreading swiftly. One of the bullets had ricocheted from the wall to strike the gleaming object. Several chunks of crystal fell to the stone floor. Steve stooped to pick up one of them. He studied it briefly before slipping it into a pocket. He looked back at the great crystal dominating the chamber. The sudden flaw from the almost-spent bullet saddened him.

Well, he thought with some satisfaction, at least I can leave here knowing we weren't the ones who did that. He slid down the shaft.

CHAPTER XXI

STEVE ANCHORED the cable securely within the cave. Wayne slid into the harness and Steve eased him down from the ledge. It was slow going because they had to work in darkness. They didn't dare chance any kind of light. When he reached the trees below, Wayne shook the cable for a signal. Steve stopped, then resumed a slow descent. Moments later the cable went slack. They waited as Wayne groped in the dark. If the copse was too small or too narrow and he fell, he was still secured in the harness. Several minutes went by, and then Steve felt three sharp jerks on the cable.

"Everything's okay below," he said. Another jerk on the cable and he hauled Wayne in swiftly. They put the harness on Carla and sent her after Wayne. The third time they sent their packs down. Rudy Wells followed. When he received the next signal, Steve grasped the cable in his left hand and slid over the ledge. He went down swiftly, slowed as he felt leaves brush his body. Then he was with them in the trees. He tied the bottom end of the cable to a tree so the wind wouldn't catch it and send it writhing into the open.

"Now what?" Rudy whispered.

"It took us five days to get here," Steve said. "Five days with eight people, heavily loaded. We were slowed by Dr. Jennings and Dr. Yavari. On the way back, well, if we go southeast we should pick up our old trail about five miles from here. We should be able to get through the grass country a lot faster this time. We won't be cutting our way through. We've got to get back to the Chalhuanca Plateau and get one of the planes."

"They might have left someone there," Wayne said.

"That's the chance we take. We have to. It would take us another week to make it from the Chalhuanca to Azul, and Fossengen could have his hired hands on the alert for us anywhere along the way. Our only hope is to make the plateau and fly out of there."

"But surely," Carla said, "those people with Fossengen won't give us the chance."

"They have no way of knowing we're not in the temple," Steve said. "We've got to stick it out where we are during the night. We can't see a thing in these trees in the dark. Chances are Fossengen will also wait until daylight to make any move, and by then we'll be well on our way. Meanwhile, if they discover we're gone they'll come after us, of course. But at least that's an if right now. We'd better sleep while we can. We may have to stay on the move day and night."

They ate lightly of rations, drank some water, and bundled up in their netting. Steve was awake an hour before first light, waiting. The moment they had enough light to start, he started down the slope. It was steep but with plenty of handholds. Two hours after getting under way they reached the edge of the valley floor. From this point on it was a matter of moving southwest until they picked up their old trail. If they made it before Fossengen realized they were gone, they'd have a lead of seven or eight miles.

Steve cinched his pack tighter, grasped the machete in his left hand. "Let's go," he said.

They made good time. At this altitude the floor beneath the trees was still comparatively free of the fierce, tangling growth they'd had to deal with on their way out of the Chalhuanca Plateau. Speed at this moment was essential; fortunately they were still rested and fresh. Steve set a vicious pace, his machete flashing back and forth whenever they encountered rough going. Mostly it was a matter of moving as fast as a steady pace would permit, ducking under branches, weaving around heavy brush. For the first three hours they drove ahead without a rest. From then on Steve gave them a ten-minute break every hour, then pushed them on. Every hour now could count for three later. They also had the advantage of being hardened from what they had already done in managing the longer trip from the Chalhuanca to Temple Mountain. Rudy Wells was down twenty pounds from what he'd been when he began the expedition. Wayne was toughened, too. Carla had behind her the experience of years working in the field.

Rudy knew what to expect from Steve—he knew the bionics capabilities of the man better than Steve himself knew—and he trusted Steve to estimate correctly the capabilities of the others. Carla had come to trust Steve totally. She had begun to be drawn to him before her father's death, and that tragedy had left her instinctively seeking the warmth of a relationship already developing. They heard no complaints from her as she kept pace with the rest of them, driving steadily across the cruel land. As for Phil Wayne, it seemed he had adopted the attitude of Mueller and Viejo before him toward this strange man Steve Austin. What he had ignored before—especially that time when Steve turned into a fury as he slashed through the high grass they'd encountered on their way to the mountain—now came home to him with sudden impact. Several times he meant to question Rudy Wells about the extraordinary person leading them, but there was never really the chance—and when they broke from their hammering pace, the need simply to rest those precious minutes overshadowed any desire for answers. Time enough later.

They were still working their way along a far-running, gentle slope. Whatever additional stamina they derived from descending into thicker air from the high point of the mountain was demanded by Steve as he took note and increased the pace. Finally they reached the long section of high grass, the last one through which they'd struggled just before reaching the slopes leading to Temple Mountain. No need now to slash and cut. Not enough time had passed for the grass to grow back. Steve took them through relentlessly and never eased off the pressure until they did begin to stumble. He had deliberately stretched their endurance to the breaking point. They would falter, he knew, but rest and food should bring them out of it, and then he would drive them just as hard until a numbness set in and they no longer would feel the stabbing aches and pains the protesting muscles would bring to them.

He gave them a break of forty-five minutes. While the others ate and drank, sprawled where they were, he prowled like an angry cat, nervous, impatient to be on his way. Carla stared at him with disbelief, and several times he caught her eyes on him and returned her frank gaze, but whatever communication she needed from him was met in this silent understanding. They were, she accepted, drawn to each other, but it was an emotion she could hardly indulge at this moment. Later, a world awaited them beyond this jungle, beyond the Chalhuanca, beyond the reach of the men no doubt coming after them from the great temple.

They were ready to move out again, on their feet, adjusting once again their pack straps. "Everyone ready?" Steve asked. They nodded or grunted in reply. Steve started to turn, to lead them on, when back in the distance he saw a sudden brilliant flash from the top of Temple Mountain.

"Look," he said quietly, pointing. They turned, the flash gone, but a huge flare of yellow-orange light was sweeping outward from the peak of the temple, from the domed chamber where they had discovered the crystal. They stared, each with his special feelings, as thick smoke boiled outward—seemingly, at this distance, at an agonizingly slow pace. They knew that what appeared to be minuscule pieces of debris to their eyes were actually massive blocks of stone. The smoke shredded before the wind. Where there had been the domed chamber, there was now empty space.

"Well, now we know," Steve said. "Move out."

Relentless, an unbroken pace, he led them into the deeper jungle, out of the sudden dips into another long section of high grass. He drove them until their eyes were glazed, let them break to eat and for an hour's rest, then dragged them again to their feet. Phil Wayne shook his head in disbelief. "Aren't we going to camp now? For tonight?"

Steve pointed at the sun near the horizon. "There's an hour, hour and a half, left of daylight. When it's light, *we move.* On your feet."

He turned and started off and they had no choice except to follow, supported only by the knowledge that he couldn't drag them more than another hour or so before the night would come. When finally he relented because of nightfall, they were grateful only for the rest. Steve watched as they dropped where they were. No one mentioned standing guard. They were too tired; they had passed all this to him. Steve went to

Carla, curled up on the ground. He placed a pack under her head, covered her securely with mosquito netting. He checked the two men, then prowled about the area. He wondered about local wildlife. He felt the weariness seep through his own body, regretted his harsh treatment of the others, knew there really was no choice. Better blisters and sore muscles than a bullet through the head like Carla's father.

He knew he couldn't sleep until one of the others was awake. He grinned as Rudy snored fitfully. It was a long way from his office or the medical laboratories, but he was proving himself here too. For the first time since they'd known each other, Rudy was being pushed to the ultimate and making it fine. Complaining, to be sure, but not faltering. Besides, he'd been talking for years about reducing the size of that bay window he carried around. Well, he'd never get a better weight-reducing program than this one.

He thought about Carla . . . not deliberately, but now that he was sitting alone, his back to a tree, the rifle across his lap and the machete nearby, his thought just went to her. He knew they were being attracted to each other as man and woman, and that if the circumstances had been different they'd have been together long before now. Carla was breaking down the walls his subconscious had thrown up against involvement. Only time would—

A deep cough came from thick growth to his left. A mountain puma. So far they'd been fortunate to have avoided one of the big cats. He remembered they were fiercely defensive about their territory. The puma had a long memory. It had probably picked up their scent when they went through here the first time and now it recognized it. Once could be ignored . . . creatures simply passing through. A second time—a possible threat to be investigated.

Steve reached for the rifle, replaced it on the ground. Too dangerous. A shot could be heard for many miles at night.

Possibly, if the wind were right, all the way across the valley to Fossengen. If Fossengen still was fairly sure they'd been killed in that explosion, he *might* not be pressing too hard in pursuit. But if he heard shots there would be no doubt and he'd be after them full speed. Fossengen surely had with him experienced, hardened trackers, men who'd spent their lives in the field. They could move with a steady, relentless pace to run down their quarry, and Steve wanted nothing to do with a firefight against professional mercenaries. The whole rationale for his punishment of these three people was to avoid just that.

Again the puma coughed, a warning sound to the intruders on its hunting grounds. Steve took up the machete in his left hand and came quietly to his feet. He knew the big cat would be coming slowly toward them from downwind. It might quarter its approach at the last, but at least Steve could judge its direction. With the blade poised in his hand, he went into a fighting crouch, the steel moving slowly before him, ready for instant striking.

Then he saw it—barely. The animal stood on a sloping rock at the edge of their camp area. It was in a partial crouch, growling softly. Steve turned slowly, his arms spreading, the machete still low but poised. Animal and man stared at one another, and by some communication the puma knew this creature would not yield *its* territory either without a fight. Glowing eyes studied Steve. The cat remembered. This other animal had been here before. It had stayed briefly, then moved away. There had been no threat to the cat's territory, no danger. The creature would go off again. No wild animal fights when it isn't necessary. If it's not threatened it will take the way of least resistance. There was no threat. The puma went off into the night.

Steve let out a long breath. The machete lowered slowly toward the ground, and he turned to replace the weapon by his pack. A sound stopped him and he quickly turned about.

"Carla! What—"

"I watched."

The sound he'd just heard *was the safety catch going back on her rifle. She'd been ready to cut down the puma if Steve were in danger . . .*

He smiled ruefully at her. "You got me covered, pardner —an old American saying." What he was feeling was old, and universal.

They awoke to a steady drizzle. All the better, thought Steve. There'd be no desire to sit on the ground and get soaked. They had no tents, no canvas covers for a windbreak or rain shelter. They ate their rations silently, drank water and were prodded to their feet. Steve waited for them, studied each in turn and then started into thickening jungle.

The world blurred for them. They were back into the vicious bog. Step-by-step they fought their way through at Steve's merciless pace. If someone slipped or faltered, a powerful arm hauled them to better footing. There was no rest. They sucked in air, ignored the insects swarming about them, numb in body and mind. Forty-five minutes rest; no more.

That night, their second, he saw what he had feared all along. He pointed it out to Rudy. Far behind them, but definitely on their trail, a tiny pinpoint of light. A fire. Fossengen and his men . . . or at least a group of the men that had trapped them for a while in the temple . . . they'd picked up their trail and were hard after them.

Steve brooded while the others slept. It had taken them five days to get from the Chalhuanca Plateau to Temple Mountain. They would need to make it back in three. They *had* to stay well ahead. They still had the long western slope to climb to reach the airplanes. That would slow them dangerously.

214

None of the three with him had the energy to stand guard while Steve slept. They needed all their strength; their sleep was critical. Steve put his back to a tree, rifle cradled in his lap, and slept like an animal ... ready at any instant to come awake, fighting.

Something woke him while it was still dark. No rain. Heavy low clouds. He scoured their camp. Nothing. He tried to rest but couldn't with his oppressive sense of foreboding. He climbed to a slope nearby, looked back along the trail they'd just traveled. And then he saw it and he understood the intimation.

A tiny gleam in darkness. Then another. Light flickering. There; again. It could be only one thing. Flashlights. Fossengen was really driving his men. Now they were tracking at night, and catching up.

Steve decided to let Rudy, Carla and Phil sleep. If he could drive them enough in the morning they could still finish the trek in the three days he'd planned. That would bring them up the slope to the plateau at nightfall. It was their only chance. He was surprised that he fell asleep. Deep, enormously refreshing. He opened his eyes as a thin sliver of gray in the eastern sky began the new day.

He woke the others. While they ate he told them about the lights he'd seen during the night. They stared at one another in disbelief. "We haven't any choice," he warned them. "We've got to make the plateau before night. If we don't ..." He shrugged.

The unseen but known force behind helped drive them. The immediate presence of Steve lashing at them kept them going when they would have fallen. The last three hours were the worst. They were climbing now, up to higher altitude—and thinner air.

They crawled and scraped their way up the last slope to the plateau, collapsed in high grass, hearts pounding. Rudy in-

215

sisted they stop briefly to eat. Their bodies called out for a chance to recoup. Steve fidgeted. He thought he'd seen movement on the trail behind them, no more than two or three miles at the most. They still had to get to one of the planes, fire it up and get off this place in the dark. It wasn't going to be easy.

They climbed wearily to their feet, moving in blackness. Steve planned to move along the northern edge of the plateau, within cover of grass and brush.

They were so close ... when Carla stopped them and pointed out the guards between them and the two planes.

CHAPTER XXII

So CLOSE, and now guards—not one or two but more like six or seven. Fossengen must have kept in contact by radio with the people he'd left behind. They were alert, carrying their rifles almost as if anticipating the chance to cut down the four who were trying to reach the airplanes.

Phil Wayne came to his side, staying low. "What do you think, Steve? We've got no cover."

Steve looked at Wayne, nodded, not answering for the moment, trying to think.

"We could get off the plateau, Steve." That from Rudy on one knee, his rifle ready. Steve wanted to laugh. The old boy was ready for a banzai charge if anyone out there made a move. But Rudy was doing some corrective thinking on his own. True, in front of them was a grim risk at best. If they backed off, they could try living off the country. Except it would take them weeks, maybe a month or more to walk out. That meant living off whatever fish they could catch or animals they might shoot. It also meant being out in the damndest jungle one could imagine while the weather around them was going to hell. And overriding all other considerations—to get off the plateau they'd have to avoid the group coming after them. No, it was here, *now,* that they would have to settle it.

Carla put her hand on Steve's arm. "A diversion, Steve?"

He turned to her, surprised. She was right. The guards were camped in the middle of the grass strip, not by the planes. Their position wasn't a bad choice, Steve realized. Whoever wanted to reach the planes after climbing the western slope, they'd figured, would have to go through them.

Except maybe not.

"Carla, those men," Steve said, gesturing to the guards, "I can't tell clearly but it seems to me they're natives. Are they?"

Wayne handed her a small pair of binoculars and she studied the scene. Reflected firelight was her only illumination but it was enough. "Yes," she told him. "Like Colonel Viejo told us. Natives, from the north country."

He thought on that, had the first glimmer of an idea. Then he slipped off his pack, began stripping to the waist. They looked at him with amazement. As he undressed he turned to Wayne. "Phil, you remember how to start that thing?"

Wayne ran through his mind the starting procedures on the C-47. "Yeah, I think so."

"There's no room for mistakes. We may have only one chance," Steve said. "You've got to do it right the first time."

"I said I remember. But why not the Helio? I mean, only one engine and—"

Steve cut him short. "The Gooney takes a lot more punishment than the Helio," Steve said, "and I'm not counting on getting out of here without those people taking a few shots at us. It may take a bit longer to get started, but our odds are better. Now just forget everything else and please stay with what I'm saying. You go along the perimeter of the field, Phil. Stay low and move fast. You've got good cover with the grass. Go around to the *other side* of the Gooney. You can see how the Helio should block their view when you come in that way, right?" Wayne nodded. "Now, *don't* use the cabin door. Drop the belly hatch and get in that way. You've got to ignore anything going on around you. Just get into that cockpit and start firing up. That's all. Get those engines running. The trick is priming them right *the first time.*" He looked at Wayne. "You may not get a second. When you've got her running, taxi out of there. Swing her around to the south and then to the other end of the strip, to the east. Come around in a wide circle and stop. If things work out, we'll be coming scared into the ship. Any questions?"

"You're kidding."

Steve clapped Wayne on the shoulder. *"Vaya con Dias,* or something."

Wayne grinned and disappeared into the night.

"Steve, would you mind telling me what you're doing?"

Steve turned to Rudy and stuffed a small package into one pants pocket before he answered. "I'm trying to think like our friends out there," he said, meaning the guards. "The only way we can hack this is, as the saying goes, to blow their minds."

"Blowing their heads off would be more like it."

"But not much chance of getting them all. There's seven of them, at least. Carla, can you see any more?"

She went back to studying the guards through the binoculars. "No, I only see seven but it's possible—"

"Okay. Now, Carla, where's that lipstick of yours?"

219

Timing would be everything. They could, as Rudy suggested, have decided to shoot it out ... four automatic rifles against seven. True, they would have had the element of surprise, but it likely wouldn't have been enough in itself to even up the odds. They'd be shooting at night into at best dim light. If even one guard survived, he could probably shoot into and destroy the planes. That they were still undamaged meant only that Fossengen had planned to use them himself. A guard trying to survive would hardly worry about Fossengen's plans. And as Carla had started to say when he'd cut her off, there was the chance there were more guards than the seven they'd seen. Some might be asleep nearby out of sight. They needed to flush out every last one of them.

Timing, *and* surprise. Catch them unawares. Hit them while they momentarily froze with surprise ... Steve went over the plan with Rudy and Carla. They synchronized their watches. It would have to be a rapid-step procedure. Wayne would get as close to the C-47 as he could without being seen, drop low and wait for the fireworks—which would be his signal to get into the airplane and get those engines going.

One element they surely couldn't control. Fossengen and his group coming up that slope. They weren't too far behind. Well, you couldn't always have *all* your ducks in a row.

Steve left his rifle behind and slipped away into darkness. He retraced their steps, staying within the grass until he reached the western end of the plateau. Now he cut south so that he could come up on the guards from the opposite side. He'd quarter his approach, keeping the guards between himself and where Rudy and Carla lay hidden in the grass. When they cut loose he didn't want to be in a straight line behind the guards. Too much lead would be flying.

He moved swiftly, running with the speed of a big cat, and as quietly. He came around in position, went prone and studied the luminous hands of his watch. About two minutes.

220

Fifteen seconds before their zero time they'd bury their faces in their arms, look anywhere but at the guards. But they'd *know* when he was moving.

He cut open his left pocket in a neat slit down the trousers, exposing his left thigh. The pressure point; he pushed down with his finger. The plastiskin panel moved away from the surface into its recess, exposing a storage tube. He reached in and removed four metal globes, each about half the size of a golf ball. He closed his leg. In the dark he felt the surface of each globe until he was certain of a ridge slightly raised from the sphere. He slipped one of the globes into a pocket, held the other three in his right hand. He'd need all the throwing power he could get, which called for the strength of his bionics arm.

He went to one knee, studied the guard camp. He took a deep breath. Quickly he stabbed down on the ridges of the spheres. Ten-second timers. As fast as he snapped the timers, he threw them. One directly in front of the guards, high over and between them and the position where Rudy and Carla waited. The second sphere to their left, the third and last to their right. He spun around, facing in the opposite direction, throwing his arm up before his eyes.

Three tiny bombs hurtled through the air in carefully timed arcs. The first exploded, a tiny *pop* lost in the night wind. There was no explosion or blast. The spheres were light bombs, compact modifications of flashbombs used by the military for night photography, and they threw out in all directions a blinding sheet of radiance—enough to take a clear photograph from five thousand feet, enough to erase sight for thirty seconds or more. Then the second and the third spheres ripped away the night.

Steve turned quickly—poised. A sudden roar came from the other side of the field. Rudy and Carla had waited, their faces buried in their arms, protecting themselves from the light. But even protected in this manner they could see something of the

221

flash destroying darkness. One, two, three, and then they were on their feet, rifles in their hands, turning about.

Seven men staggered to their feet, hands at their eyes. Rudy and Carla began firing off thirty-round clips. Three, then five men were knocked from their feet as the high-velocity rounds smacked into them. Another went down. The seventh was firing blindly, a reflex action, in the general direction of his unseen attackers.

Rudy and Carla were to fire until their clips were empty. Each now had one clip left. Their instructions were to empty the clips, then eject the empties and insert their last clips. Now Steve would make his move.

He started running, staying low, the machete gripped tightly in his left hand. And he saw that his fears were realized. Three men came running from a low tent Carla hadn't seen. They ran into the night, startled, but also angry and ready. They'd seen the flashes of the guns from across the field, and immediately crouched or went flat, returning the fire.

Steve ran with all the speed he could bring to his bionics limbs, steel feet thudding into the ground, closing on the remaining guards. He timed it by an expectation of their reflexes. He bellowed as loud as he could. The guards, startled again, turned their heads.

In the flickering light of their fire they saw what surely seemed some sort of demon, a white savage with red stripes across face and body. He came at them with unexpected speed. They were bringing their guns to bear, turning as fast as they could, but Steve was already in their midst. His machete came about in a terrible slash as it ripped into a shoulder, carrying entirely through the chest. No time to hesitate. Steve kept moving, pivoting on those pistonlike legs, the machete coming back now in a backswing that took the second man at the waist. Again blood sprayed in the reflection of firelight as the man fell to the side.

The third guard stared at the apparition that had emerged

so violently from the darkness. His rifle sounded but it was without aim. Steve threw himself at the man, unable to bring the machete to bear at such close quarters. He hit the man with a stunning blow of his own body. The machete fell from his hand as he brought up his arm, bionics fist closed in a steel bludgeon. The blow crushed the man's skull.

Steve dropped to the ground and rolled to the side. There was still that one guard from the first group. He hadn't seen him fall. A gun fired and bullets ripped into the ground, tearing into and over the body of the man Steve had killed with his fist. Steve continued rolling. The guard was too far for Steve to go for him. The man was still effective with his weapon, and he was trying to catch Steve for just that one moment needed to cut him down.

Another burst of fire, but this time from across the field. The guard stumbled from the impact as lead went through him. He fell without a sound.

Steve came to his feet, running. No one else moved. He took off across the field to where he'd left Rudy and Carla, whom he saw now on her feet, rifle barrel smoking. Carla had been ready to save his life once before. Likely now she had finally done it.

"Steve, quickly . . . Rudy's been hit." She pointed to where Rudy lay on the ground, hands gripping his right leg. Even in the darkness Steve saw the dull shine of fresh blood. He dropped beside Rudy, gritting his teeth with pain, trying not to cry out.

"No time to stop it now," Rudy said. "I saw something at the end of the field." Steve turned his head. In the distance, just coming up the last slope to the plateau, moving figures. If they were ever going to make it . . .

He bent down, pulled Rudy roughly from the ground and got him over his shoulder. "The plane . . . run for it," he told Carla.

She did, and Steve began to outdistance her despite his

burden. He heard Rudy gasp with pain from the pounding but there was no help for it. Ahead of them an engine coughed to life, then roared as Wayne caught it with a sure touch at the throttle. Steve was mentally urging Wayne on, going through the starting procedures. He heard the second prop turning over, coughing, stopping, then catching. A sudden blast of power. *Not too hard, play it, play it* . . . The roar increased as Wayne brought power to both engines and the C-47 rolled ahead, then swung to the left, the right engine thundering as Wayne brought in more power to turn her. They were coming together. They reached the C-47, ran toward the tail. The blast of air from the props nearly tumbled Steve as he went for the belly hatch.

He heaved, then shoved Rudy through the hatch and out of the way. Carla was by his side. "Get in," Steve shouted at her. She reached up to the edge of the hatch and he grabbed her by the waist, half-lifting and half-throwing her into the cabin behind Rudy.

Something smacked into metal by his head. They were getting the range. . . . He heaved himself into the cabin, saw Carla by Rudy, well away from the open hatch. He rushed up the cabin to the cockpit. Wayne turned to him, clearly and appropriately terrified. But he knew how to keep his head. He was in the right seat, and Steve clambered into the left, not bothering with the belt. He hit the throttles, bringing the transport around, pointing down the grass strip. All he could see were tiny orange flashes as Fossengen and his men directed their fire at the airplane.

They had to get past a dozen automatic rifles firing at close range. Steve didn't know the direction of the wind, and at this altitude unless they had everything working for them, he'd never get the ship off the ground before they were out of runway.

The rockets. He'd forgotten all about them. He reached

224

down as they started to roll, tore away the safety wire. "Phil, when I call it out, hit this switch!" He couldn't fire the RATO bottles too soon. The rockets burned only so long and they had to be timed exactly right for best effect. The engines went to full throttle. They rolled forward, painfully slow in their acceleration. He had to stay with it. He knew Fossengen's men were fanning out, ready to catch them in a crossfire as they went past.

They ducked as metal shattered along the side of the plane's nose. They were getting the range. The plane could be taken out at any moment. If only he could—

The last sphere. In his pocket. "Hold her steady," he shouted to Wayne. Phil grabbed the yoke and hung on. They had enough speed to bring up the tail, get rid of some of their drag, roll along on the main gear only. Steve pulled open the window by his side. He had the sphere in his hand, stabbing on the timer release. His left hand, into the wind. He threw, as hard as he could, straight ahead.

"Cover your eyes," he told Wayne. "I've got her." He grabbed the yoke, corrected slightly with the rudder. He was counting. He hung on. The exploding flashbomb gutted the night. No more firing. The flashbomb had done it. Fossengen's men, blind for the moment, staggering back as if struck.

Time now for the rocket boosters. "Phil, the switch. Hit it!"

Nothing. He had braced himself for the rockets. Nothing! Angrily he turned to Wayne, froze. The windshield on the right was gone, shattered. He had time only for a glimpse of a bloody mess, then his right hand went down to the switch, cracked it into position.

A glare spread about them, raced in all directions from the accelerating transport as the solid rockets lit. Flame rushed back as a special force took hold of the C-47, pushed it forward faster and faster. There were no cockpit lights. Steve couldn't even see the airspeed indicator. It didn't matter. He put everything on the flaming blast of those rockets. He came back gently on the yoke and felt the vibration from the gear end. Steve brought up the gear, rolled at once into a left turn, ready to drop the nose. His hand sought the panel light switch. The instruments suddenly glowed at him.

The transport shuddered as the rockets cut out. He went forward on the yoke. The turn would have brought them to the left of the plateau, to the south, clear of that sheer drop of several thousand feet. Empty space—blessed open air to let the nose drop, the speed pick up. The needle on the airspeed dial came steadily around. Steve punched the jettison switch. He felt the slight jar as the empty rocket bottles were pushed away from the belly. The speed picked up still more. Steve leaned back in the seat, fighting to recover.

He turned to Phil and froze. That last burst that took out the windshield had been nearly fatal. Phil sagged against the side of the cockpit. Steve leaned over, turned on the overhead chart light so that it played on the unconscious man. The blood had stopped. The cold. The cold had kept Phil alive, helped staunch the flow of blood. Steve worked the copilot's oxygen mask from its rack, slipped it over Phil, turned the flow to 100 percent oxygen. He felt the man's pulse. Weak, but he would hold for a while. Until they got past those high peaks . . .

Steve sagged in his seat at the controls, flying by rote, easing the C-47 in a steady climb over the mountains. Lima lay straight ahead.

He remembered finally to bring the oxygen mask to his own face. Remembered, also, the two people in the cabin behind him. Realized, suddenly with wicked impact, that the temperature was below zero and that he was bare to the waist. He locked in the automatic pilot, switched to the walk-around oxygen bottle and climbed stiffly from his seat. He was shivering with the bitter cold as he went back into the cabin. He groped for the cabin light switch, flicked it on. Piled against equipment bags were the still forms of Carla and Rudy.

Steve hurried to them, pausing only long enough to drag the hatch cover from where Phil had tossed it, and slipped it into place. At least that stopped the freezing windblast.

They were unconscious. Steve grabbed two masks from their racks, turned the flow to 100 percent oxygen, held them against the faces of Carla and Rudy. It would take a little while. Clumsy, half-frozen, he slipped the straps over their heads. He stopped to turn on the cabin heater switch to maximum. On his way back to the cockpit he grabbed a blanket lying on top of an equipment pack, wrapped it about him. Hell of a flight suit, but it would do. In the cockpit he checked Phil again. Unconscious or sleeping. Probably in shock, but he should hold until they got back to the ground. Steve fastened the seat belt around Phil, then got the shoulder harness hooked up and the inertial reel locked. If Phil suddenly came out of it, he wouldn't be able to flail around and hurt himself or the airplane. Steve made a quick check of the gauges. She was holding steady. He made a minor adjustment to the power settings, and went to the rear again.

Carla was groping clumsily to sit up. She nodded to tell him she was coming out of it. He turned to Rudy. Thank God, he was breathing, and around his leg above the wound was a tourniquet. Carla had managed that before she passed out. He moved Rudy to a more comfortable position, raised his head slightly and waited. He began to stir several minutes later. Steve made sure the mask was on properly. Rudy came back to full consciousness in great pain. He was still the doctor, but it must have felt strange to be telling someone else what to do about his leg. There was a first-aid kit in the cockpit. Steve brought it back, did as he was told.

No wonder he'd heard Rudy gasping with pain before. The leg was broken. He gave Rudy a shot of morphine, then told him and Carla what had happened, where they were. The drug was affecting Rudy. He nodded his understanding, then gave in to the spreading effect of the morphine.

"He'll sleep for a while," Steve told Carla. She nodded, looking at him. "Watch him, will you?"

"Of course . . ." She reached out for his hand and he held hers. No need for words now. Their eyes met in a silent promise. Later.

Steve went back to the cockpit, still painted, returned to the controls. He turned on the radios but waited before using them. He needed a few moments to himself. He looked at Phil. Without him . . .

He looked ahead. Up here the stars were bright and clear, the heavy clouds far beneath them. There was a moon somewhere. He could see the dim glow in the sky.

He thought about the film in his pocket. Phil had also managed to save the film he carried with him. It had been bought with blood and lives. But there was much more than the film. That piece of the crystal he'd picked up when the stray bullet ricocheted into and despoiled the gleaming surface. It could be the key. He pictured the now destroyed huge crystal in his mind and saw it reborn and thought of what it could do and what it meant. With the films and his small piece scientists could possibly create its duplicate, bring it back to life.

He thought of the stories that had pursued the mysteries of the past. And the ancients who had peopled those dim and cloudy centuries so long ago. With all they had just been through, what they had seen and what they had discovered, could one still shrug off even the most bizarre claims? Were the chariots of the gods and strange visitations to this world really such far-fetched notions as some claimed, or were they part of an unbreakable thread of reality? Not so very long ago the idea of the crystal had precious little substance. . . .

More tired than he'd realized, he eased the nose down, starting the long descent for Lima. He called in to air traffic control, told them position and time out from landing, asked for an ambulance to be waiting. And would they notify the American embassy. There'd be questions to be answered, and he was too tired to bother.

Now he wanted to think only about Carla. And himself. How things would take care of themselves, if given the chance.

He came out of the night sky, a great metal ghost. The wheels touched and he bled off the speed, letting the tail slide to the ground. He taxied to the flight line, swung her around smartly, locked the brakes. He shut her down, flicking switches.